Singing Her Alive

A Fictional Memoir

By Diana K. Perkins

Leah —
Enjoy!
Diana K. Perkins
June 30, 2012

Copyright © 2011 by Diana K. Perkins
First Edition – August 2011

ISBN
978-1-77067-118-8 (Hardcover)
978-1-77067-119-5 (Paperback)
978-1-77067-120-1 (eBook)

Readers: Eve Brehenne, Barbara Doak, Sheilagh Garrity, Laura Lawrence, Christine Pattee, Susan Sharin, Brooke Shannon

Edited by: Cheryl Gagne

Published by:

FriesenPress
Suite 300 – 852 Fort Street
Victoria, BC, Canada V8W 1H8

www.friesenpress.com

Distributed to the trade by The Ingram Book Company

Table of Contents

Author's Note

This novel is sited in Willimantic, Connecticut and the surrounding towns of the Willimantic River valley. Willimantic was a thriving mill town during the time when the older story is set, in the late 1800's, early 1900's, and some of the buildings from the period still survive including the Elms boarding house and the third floor Library of the mill store, now housed in the Willimantic Textile Mill and History Museum. Please see the addendum for more information on history and era of the mill girls.

For pictures and more history on the Company store and Workers Library housed therein, visit the website:

http://www.millmuseum.org/Mill_Museum/Captains_of_Ind.html.

Disclaimer

This is a fictional memoir; any resemblance to actual lives or persons is purely accidental and should not be taken as fact.

Acknowledgments

I want to thank my faithful readers who with encouragement and support helped me to bring this novel to fruition, including, Eve Brehenne, Sheilagh Garrity, Christine Pattee, Laura Lawrence, Barbara Doak, Susan Sharin and Brooke Shannon. A special thanks to editor, Cheryl Gagne. Many thanks to the FriesenPress Account Manager, Caroline Johns, who patiently led me through the publishing process, and to my sweet and thorough editor, Caroline H. Davidson.

To Michelle

Sarah:

This is our story.

Three generations.

Each one is as different as the root, the vine and the leaf.

Bear with me as I untwine the tangled vine.

And search for the hidden truths that lie within.

Chapter 1 – Sarah

Like an out of body experience, I see myself walking down this dirt road, far from the main road. I try to imagine what it must be like to live in one place all of your life. My grandmother Rebecca did it. I have come back here to bury her. She said she lived here for 60 years, and my mother grew up here.

I stumble on a rock and curse my luck and my damned car for getting a flat a half mile back. Even frustrated about the flat, I can't help soaking up the quiet, the beauty, and the loveliness of the spot. The dappling of leaf shadows on the dirt road with the grass growing up in the middle, the stone walls paralleling the road, the old maples growing along the walls and tumbling them with their slow growth, the fields beyond. It is at once familiar and yet foreign. My heart gives a leap as the house comes into view, just as it had every time I came to visit. The two- story white farmhouse with the long porch that spans its full breadth is my warm, embracing, and welcoming past. It hides its history in flowers and old lace. How is it possible that on this trip I will find under the dried flowers and dusty lace, family secrets so shocking that I will never again trust the façade of the wholesome family picture? For the rest of my life I will watch for little telltale signs of the drama that lies beneath.

I take a deep breath as I pause on the road to soak it up, the calm of the country. All the stress of the traffic, the ride, the city, the work, and my aggravation with Mom, starts to fall away. It seems strange to be returning to this place filled with so many memories, knowing that the people who were the larger part of those memories are gone. Why hadn't I come back more often, visited more than once or twice a year? I loved this place and the people.

I was annoyingly roused from these thoughts as a car came up from behind me and honked twice. My mother, Beatrice, drives by. She's smiling, waving, raising dust and pulling into the driveway. She got out and stood there as I walked up, with her hands on her hips looking back at me.

"Well, what took you so long?" she called in her usual confrontational manner. "That car of yours break down again?"

"It's only broken down once before, and it's all I can afford. And hi to you, too." I said, trying not to get caught up in our usual verbal sparring. "And besides, it's a flat. That hardly counts as a breakdown."

Bea shrugged, and turned towards the house with her big bunch of keys jangling.

I pause at the gardens, once so impressive. Even though it's early spring, they are wildly overgrown with weeds. When Grandpa Pete was alive it always looked beautiful: peonies, woodruff, irises, phlox, lavender, and hollyhocks all in abundance. On hot summer days the air was humming with bees and heavy with fragrance. There were small tomatoes among the flowers, yellow ones shaped like little pears and a red cherry variety. Grandpa Pete would send me out with the salt shaker to have all I wanted – they were warm and sweet and the juice ran down my chin. Ma said he got a kick out of me, liked that I was so strong and tough acting and how I wouldn't take guff from anyone. He told her I would get along just fine in the world and that coddling me wouldn't help me, that it didn't help anyone.

Pete was always good for an opinion about how to raise children. They raised Bea, he would say, and she turned out just fine too. "Maybe a little spoiled" Pete said about her, "Couldn't help it though, she was our only child".

"You coming in here to help or are you gonna stand around out there forever, daydreaming?" Bea was relentless; if I wasn't helping or giving her my full attention, she would cause a ruckus.

I stepped up the stairs to the porch, noticing that the banister was a little shaky. When Pete was alive the place was always kept up, no loose banisters, no chipping paint, no tall grass creeping up to the porch edge. Well, at least not while he was still able. It was hard to watch him deteriorate, get weak and tender. He would repeat the mantra that it was hard to get old, as though one should not do it if it could be avoided.

But, Grandma Becky and Aunt Doris, the housekeeper, took good care of him as he declined and even tried to keep the house and garden up. In the garden, he nagged them relentlessly, and because he couldn't do it himself, he would order them around and survey their every task, telling them how it should be done and how he wished he could do it. Finally they would lose patience and tell him to go into the house or they would not do another thing, and he would turn slowly around with his walker and go sputtering back into the house.

When I opened the front door, my eye went directly up the stairs to the second floor, the wide banister polished from years of wear, was my favorite for sliding down. Pete held me when I was smaller, but once I got big enough and was able to climb onto it myself, he would watch me slide down, run up the stairs and slide down again in an endless circle. The stairway divided the house. On the right was a hall with several rooms off it. On the left were the living room and the parlor and behind that the kitchen – the hall met the kitchen in the back with a little pantry and then a washroom.

Bea was unpacking a box in the kitchen as I walked in through the parlor. The smell of Old struck me like a physical force: old wool carpets where the dog urine could not quite be cleaned out, stale dry flowers no longer fragrant, musty basement creeping up through the floor, something sour of undeterminable origin. The living room and parlor were dark with the heavy drapes closed. I yelled to Bea in the kitchen, "Mind if I open some windows? It's kinda stinky in here"

"No problem, Honey. It's smelled like that for years now. I don't think they could quite keep up with that old Irish setter."

The old pressed glass candy dish still had butterscotches in it. When I clinked the top and crinkled the wrapper while taking one out, Bea called out, "Hey you into those candies already? I can't believe it, they must be ancient. We couldn't keep you out of them when you were a kid." They were ancient, sticky goo oozed from the cellophane, requiring me to lick my fingers after I popped it into my mouth.

"Is the phone still working? I want to call a garage to fix that flat."

"Yep, I haven't had time to have it turned off – try Mason's garage, in the phone book there – it's close and fair, and they know us." Bea worried about those things, like whether or not a company knew you and you knew them. She set a lot of store by that; she said it was Pete's influence. She said no one is going to cheat you in a small town because everyone would hear about it and shortly they'd be out of business.

I phoned the garage, and then drew back the drapes from the parlor windows, banged at the sticking sash and drew it open. I went into the main floor bedroom to do the same and get some cross ventilation going. The main floor bedroom was where Pete stayed as he got older and couldn't negotiate the stairs. I always remembered him staying in there. It was at the bottom of the stairs, the first room on the hall that ran to the back of the house. The room still looked the same. Pictures of Pete and Becky dressed up, maybe getting married with Aunt Doris in attendance and some other guy I didn't recognize. Aunt Doris wasn't my real aunt, but that's what we always called her.

"Gee, Mom, I didn't know that they knew Aunt Doris that long. I thought they met when they hired her after Grandma couldn't keep up."

As I walked into the kitchen, Bea had just finished unpacking the box of cleaning supplies. She opened the refrigerator and let out a little disgusted puff of breath.

"Hand me that baking soda, ok, Hon?" She donned her yellow rubber gloves and took out a sponge, wet it from the sputtering faucet and started to wipe down the fridge.

"I emptied this out when Mom went into the hospital, but I never got a chance to clean it."

She leaned in and pulled out a shelf and handed it to me. I put it into the old chipped white porcelain sink and started to rinse it off. The view from the window above the sink was bright and green with lawn and garden extending outward and then dropping down the hill to what was once a large vegetable garden. It was strange looking out this window into the yard. When I was little, I would tug on Aunt Doris's apron asking to be held up to spy on the birds hovering around the feeder. Now, I'm the tall one looking out of the window. Now, I'm the one seeing the missing putty and chipped paint.

Once the refrigerator was, by Bea's standards, "reasonably clean", she went to the bag on the kitchen table and stocked the fridge with cold cuts and sodas and some fruit that we could have while we were working on the task of sorting through the rooms full of their possessions. I wandered through the house, going into rooms that before now I would not have been allowed in or would have avoided out of respect.

The rooms were not cluttered, but the task ahead still seemed over-whelming. I went upstairs to Rebecca's room. I wasn't sure where to start. I pulled open a dresser drawer and found a white full-length slip with lace bodice that looked as if it was brand new, and a thin flat box under it with tissue and another slip, pink, that was definitely brand new.

All the old adages about wearing that new dress and dancing like there was no tomorrow came back to me. Why do we save those favorite things? Why don't we use them or wear them? Is it part of a gamble, or a faith in the future, that there will be a time when we will be dancing again? I made another solemn vow not to do that, to just wear that beautiful red cashmere sweater that Joe got for me, even though it might shrink, and his stubborn streak might not.

Bea stuck her head in the door, "Let's make a plan before we get started. Maybe then we can avoid spending too much time reminiscing instead of making the hard decisions. That way we can try to get through this before you have to go back to work."

Bea was good at lists and organizing. Sometimes it annoyed the hell out of me. And when I didn't always go along with her plans, just because I wanted to do things my way once in a while, it would turn out that her way usually proved to be better, but sometimes I didn't care.

"Come on down, I've got a couple of pads of paper and I can show you where some keys and secret closets are." Bea turned around and went down the stairs and I followed.

In the smaller parlor where I'd opened the drapes, the light streamed in and filtered down through the dusty air. Grandma called it the small parlor but I think it was originally intended to be a dining room since it was closest to the kitchen in the back of the house, and it wasn't a grand house that would have more than one parlor. Bea had set up the side table with two sodas, some peanut butter crackers and the pads and pencils. Before Bea could sit down she was compelled to straighten an old print of a river meandering through autumn woods. She just couldn't stand to have some things out of place. Once straightened, the brighter pattern of the wallpaper showed in an off-kilter rectangle behind it.

"I guess that wallpaper will have to go. I wonder if we can just leave it and hope that the realtor won't insist we re-wallpaper the room," Bea mused. We sat in the two overstuffed chairs next to the table; one had been Grandma's and one had been Aunt Doris's. I could still imagine them sitting there. And when I would go to visit, I can still see Grandma rocking a little to push herself out of the chair as she came over to greet me. The little arm covers with straight pins holding them in place were gently stained with oil from their hands and long use. These days, people would just throw the old chairs out and buy new.

Bea handed me a pad. "OK, how does this sound. We each take a room; we go through it top to bottom. We want to have it totally empty by the end of the week if we can, so everything goes. Either it goes into the garbage, into a pile for the auction, into a pile for the local shelter or one of us can take it if there is anything we want. Big furniture pieces we'll worry about later. What do you think?"

Bea was getting shrewd in her middle age. She knew if she just dictated to me, I wouldn't go along, but now she's giving me choices so that I would feel included in the decision making process. She should have used that tactic on me when I was a child.

"Sounds good, where are the piles for auction and local shelter going to be located?"

Bea nodded and smiled, "How about near the front door in the living room? Auction stuff on the right, shelter stuff on the left. We can bring as much of the light furniture as we can carry down into the living room, and leave the big stuff for the auction guys. We'll call them when we're ready. There are some boxes in the back of the car we can use to collect some of the other stuff and here's a marker so we will know which is which."

"Ma, you are always two steps ahead." Bea smiled and looked pleased with herself. I couldn't help thinking that less than a week ago she'd lost her mother. How did she do it, how did she seem so cool and detached, as though it happened years ago, or as if it was someone else's mother?

She sipped on the soda, popped a couple of crackers into her mouth and after swallowing once and taking another sip of soda said, "You can take Pete's room. I'll take Rebecca's and then we can both work on Aunt Doris's."

"No, I think I want Rebecca's room. There might be something in there that I want, you know, a keepsake from her. Do you mind? Would it be ok if I worked on her room?"

"Oh, I guess. But if you find anything that I might want, hold it out for me." There was a slight note of disappointment in her voice, but she wasn't going to challenge me on it.

"Of course I will," I said as I headed up the stairs.

"Don't forget the boxes."

"Right."

I turned around, went out to the driveway and pulled four nested boxes out of her back seat. I dropped off two inside Pete's door before I started to climb the stairs, little knowing that I was heading into a family drama that would change my life.

Chapter 2 – Sarah

I started out as we had agreed, in Rebecca's room. After doing a slow 360 degree turn in the center of the room, I decided to begin with the closet, pulling out an armload of dresses and laying them on the bed. A quick browse through them showed they should probably go to the shelter, as none of them were even remotely in style or something Bea or I would wear. I doubted anyone at the shelter or Salvation Army would be interested, except to use them for costumes or quilts.

Back in the closet I shuffled through more dresses, some sweaters, a couple of coats and jackets, nothing of importance, but at the far back, there was an old fox stole with the fox head and paws. It felt a little stiff with age and looked a little moth eaten, but was a fun piece and if mom didn't want it, I might. Boxes on the closet shelf held shoes, crochet hooks, knitting needles, knitting books, and bags of yarn. A box on the floor held pictures. I put it on the bed, thinking it would be fun to poke through them with Mom during the week.

Most of the stuff went to the shelter pile, but the crochet hooks, knitting needles and yarn could go to a rummage sale. I'd have to ask Bea if she was planning one. On Rebecca's dresser were some pretty perfume bottles. A couple of them had cut glass stoppers and one a rubber squeeze atomizer. These might be saleable, but I thought I would keep one of the cut glass bottles for myself. There was also a jewelry box, which primarily held costume jewelry, with one nice, though well-worn gold bracelet. It was set with a large oval amethyst. I put it aside for Bea. Another gem lay within the junk. Near the bottom was a small, gold-plated and bejeweled, scimitar broach set with semi precious stones; something from a bygone era. Last on top of the dresser was a fine ivory comb, brush and mirror set that might fetch a pretty good price at the auction, that is if Bea wasn't interested.

Sometimes it felt so mercenary, looking over all these dear possessions and deciding what to keep and what to sell, divorcing myself from the reality of their ownership.

The small top drawers of the dresser hid a nice little manicure set and a tin box holding old silver quarters and half dollars. I continued to ruminate about things that people accumulate during their lives that just pile up like so much debris that has to be sorted through and distributed. These are the items that they used in their daily lives, or treasured, or for some other reason, couldn't part with. So many people collect useless things because they think it's wasteful to toss them out: plastic bags, rubber bands, paper clips, pens that don't write anymore, scraps of paper, and watches that haven't worked for decades. What is it about us that we accumulate these things? Rebecca wasn't bad about collecting useless or peculiar things; in fact, she was somewhat Spartan in her personal items. Maybe a few more hankies or pink slips than one might normally own, but I didn't open a closet and have a hundred rolls of toilet paper fall out on me. There was one ancient corset, and garter belt, but no grand accumulation of old or odd items.

The dresser and bureau and bed would probably go for a fair price too, they looked like mahogany and had some nice carved details and several cedar-lined drawers, a classic design in good condition. There was an old vanity with drawers on both sides and side mirrors that folded in, enabling one to get good side good views while primping.

I was halfway through the vanity drawers when Bea called up the stairs, "Come on down. Time to break for lunch."

I hadn't realized how long we'd worked or how hungry I was. When I got down to the kitchen, Bea already had the sandwich bread out, lettuce torn up and was slicing tomatoes.

"Get the ham and salami and cheese from the fridge, ok? Just because we're out here in the middle of nowhere, doesn't mean we can't eat well."

"This isn't nowhere, Ma. It's not that far to town, it probably just seemed like it when you were a kid. Now that things are getting so built up, well it's only a few miles to a store." I pulled the packets of cold cuts from the fridge. As if to underscore my point, at that moment, a car flew by the house, stirring up a cloud of dust.

The old house was at the junction of another road with five other houses that seemed like a small village, on the edge of a large farm. Only about a mile away was a little mill and the old railroad depot, the train tracks running along by the river. For some reason this little village didn't thrive as some had, but remained an isolated little crop of homes. There was new growth in the area so that the little village was getting closer and closer to a busier community. Farms were getting bought up and houses popped up like mushrooms on the old farmland, and a strip mall here and there. I was sad to see that lifestyle go, the big farms broken up, knowing that with it, went a way of life. I'm sure I romanticized farming, but it seemed so right, so healthy, that simple farm life.

Another car went by and I looked up from my sandwich making.

"What was it like to grow up here?"

"Well, it felt safe, not like nowadays when people seem afraid to let their kids walk to school. We really did walk to school back then. It felt peaceful, too. Your grandma and I would sit out on the back stoop in the evening, watching the sun go down and listening to the robin's evening song. Ma always liked thunderstorms and she would sit out on the porch and watch them and after a few good cracks of lightning, the rain would pour out of the sky as if out of a bucket, coming down so hard the mist from it would blow back on us sitting on the porch swing. One hot day we were sitting on the porch and I saw a big black snake curled up in the bushes and the surprise of it scared me. I hollered, and out came Dad. He grabbed that snake by the tail before it could get away, and snapped it like a whip and broke its neck. I was really upset by that, I thought the snake was harmless and shouldn't have been hurt. Mom and Dad thought I was crazy, they didn't understand me. They just laughed at me, and I was hurt by that." She paused, and in a gesture that was so familiar to me ran her fingers through her short, thick hair, once dirty blonde, now graying. She gave me a quirky half smile and picked up her sandwich.

"I was always an animal lover, and in a rural farming community, an animal lover is considered silly and overly sensitive. But overall, growing up here was really good. Ma loved me in her way, Dad loved me in his way and Aunt Doris loved me in her own way, so I generally felt I was pretty lucky. Aunt Doris was probably the one who most understood my soft spot for critters and she would sometimes help me hide a wild thing I was trying to rescue. It took me many years to realize that nature does what is best and trying to fix every injured little animal is not always in its best interest."

"Weren't you lonely, Ma?" It seemed to me that the tiny village was just too quiet and dead for children to learn to socialize in.

"It wasn't that bad and I didn't know any better. Uncle Willie and Mike were next door, and the Wilsons and their two kids just a few houses down and then there were the Whites. They were in the farm about a quarter mile down around the bend, and they had four kids. I got along all right, I guess, and then, when I went to school there were plenty of kids, just like me, from out of the way places, like wild kittens, just learning to get over their shy ways."

We had finished up our sandwiches and were picking up when Bea, with her perfect timing said, "So, how's Joe doing?" She knew that we'd broken up six months back and then had gotten back together. She also knew it was kind of shaky. She never liked him much, but she did want to see me find the right person and maybe get married. She was worried I'd make it into my forties without something stable or permanent. I didn't like for her to pressure me and she knew that too.

"He's fine, just fine." I hoped it was obvious that was all I was going to say and any further pushing right now would only create a row. Thankfully a tow truck pulled into the driveway behind Bea's car and beeped. I went out to meet the truck and ride along to my car to get the flat fixed. I was surprised to find the tow truck mechanic was a woman, baseball cap pulled low, pony tail out the back and with little gold earrings. She smiled as I climbed in, and chatted easily as we drove to my car, talking about how some people reacted when she would arrive.

"This one time, an older guy, refused to let me tow the car. He told me to call the garage and have them send someone else. I called the garage using his phone. Ralph got on, Ralph Mason, he's my boss and owns the garage, and he told him that either he would let me tow the car, or he could call another garage." She chatted through the whole process of jacking the car up, plugging the hole and shouting over the air compressor as she filled the tire.

In no time it was fixed, I tipped her and thanked her for the repair and the entertainment; she laughed at that. Back at Grandma's I parked behind Bea's car and brought more boxes in.

I headed back up the stairs and started to finish off the vanity. Sorting through the top right drawer I found hairpins, old spoolies, scraps of cotton balls, old, worn down lipsticks and a couple of samples of Avon face cream. The only thing in the middle drawer was a box that looked like a ring box. I opened it, thinking it must have been Rebecca's wedding band. I tried it on. It fit perfectly, but I put it aside for Bea. In the last, bottom drawer there were some more hankies, and beneath them, a book, a diary. It was an old school exercise book and on the front it had Rebecca's initials, RM. The handwriting was at first cautious, as though it was for school exercises and the writer was conscious of penmanship. The ink was spattered in spots as though written with a fountain pen or maybe a dipped crow quill. It was a diary of her daily life, a window into her youth.

Chapter 3 – Rebecca

April 18, 1891

The umbrella man came today. Ma had several umbrellas for him to fix. He took one of them, shook his head, but still went back to his wagon and in 10 minutes came back with it fixed. "Good as new," he said. When he saw the second one, he just shook his head and told Ma it couldn't be fixed. He happened to have two new ones that he said he could trade for her old umbrella and two bits. She said she couldn't do that and would just keep the broken one.

Then he said, "Wait. Just let me look at it again. Oh yes, it's not a broken rib, just the hinge has been lost." He pushed it in front of her face so she could inspect it, and said "See? I can fix this in a jiffy," and skittered back to his wagon. True to his word, he returned with the fixed umbrella.

"Ten cents for each," he said, smiling and shifting his weight from foot to foot. Ma went back inside, and I could hear the rattle of a tin with coins in it being opened. She returned with the twenty cents and two warm muffins.

"Here you go, and thank you for fixing them." He grinned through several days of white whisker stubs, one front tooth missing, then turned and went back to his wagon.

May 1, 1891

My sister and I hung a May basket on the Haskell's door and one also on the Grady's. I went out early in the morning to pick the flowers, and Mom found some baskets to arrange them in. Then we all went to Haskell's for cookies and tea and a Maypole. We danced with our ribbons and twined back and forth weaving in and out until we fell down exhausted and giggling.

May 9, 1891

The butcher came through in his wagon today and gave all the kids who followed him around a hotdog from the string of links he had hanging in the wagon. Ma bought a big smoked ham. We were all looking forward to a good ham dinner on Sunday, and then the ham and bean soup she would make after that. We were busy going through the pile of old clothes trying to figure out if any of them were good for a quilt or a rug before they went into the ragbag, and then to the ragman who Ma expected in the next week or two.

June 14, 1891

We all went to the pond today. Mom packed a picnic and we spread blankets and we picnicked and watched the people around us swimming and going out in little boats and fishing. After a while Ma let me wade around in the shallows and of course I fell in – she probably expected it when she told me to wear my old clothes. It was fun but by the time we got home I was chilled to the bone, and still had to go feed the chickens.

June 19, 1891

The gypsies came through today. I didn't get a good look at them. Jerry ran down the road shouting that they were coming and the women ran out to take their laundry in and the men rushed to pick up loose garden tools and bring their animals into the barns. Most families brought the little kids in and closed their doors, windows and curtains. I heard a wagon come through, rattling like the tin man's at every step of the horse and bump in the road. The little village must have looked deserted to them, probably like most villages looked upon their arrival. I peeped out through a crack in the curtain and saw a man driving a wagon with two mules pulling it. A strange affair, it looked like a huge, wildly painted rain barrel lying on its side. The mules wore brightly decorated bridles with dirty red tassels dangling from them. The man was dark and rough-looking. He yelled something and a child poked his head out from the curtains of the wagon, jumped off and ran a little way. Then he grabbed a chicken by its legs as it tried to run away. The chicken squawked and then Ma hollered at me to close the curtains. The child had been dark and dirty-looking, just like the man driving the wagon. Lydia said they camped outside the other end of town and she could hear them arguing loudly, and later she heard singing and music.

July 15, 1891

The table boarders had met with friends at the tavern and came to dinner smelling like alcohol. Ma sometimes put up with these indiscretions even on Sundays, just as long as they weren't too rowdy or it didn't happen too often. They were a pretty good lot, and would often help Pa with a heavy chore like lifting a wagon to get a new wheel on. So a little silliness, as Ma put it, was sometimes overlooked. One time they helped butcher a pig, since it's such a big job. It was welcome to have extra hands to winch the carcass up over the scalding barrel. Of course they knew there would be extra bacon or sausages out of it. Most of them slept in one of the mill houses together, several to a room. When I was really little I had a crush on one of them, Antony, the dark haired one who walked with a limp because he got kicked by a horse. The next person I got a crush on was... oh, I can't say here. If Ma ever read this, she'd have a hissy fit.

Sept. 14, 1891

We're back to school. Miss Smith let me ring the school bell today. Charlie Partick got into trouble when he asked to go out to the backhouse and Miss Smith told him to wait until the class was over. He stood up several times, asking to go out and each time Miss Smith, getting more and more annoyed, told him to sit down and wait. Finally he stood up and the pee ran right down his leg, into his shoe and onto the floor. Miss Smith was livid, and sent him home. I bet he got the switch when he got home.

Oct. 31, 1891

On Halloween we went to Wilson's to dunk for apples and to carve pumpkins. They gave us strong cider and donuts. On the way home I could hear the shouts of boys in the neighborhood going around and tipping outhouses, hollering and laughing in the dark, scattering the Sears and Roebuck Catalogue pages to the wind. If for some reason the family had crossed one of the troublemakers, they would conspire together to move the outhouse to a major thoroughfare. Last year they moved the Worthington's to the green and put a scarecrow that remarkably resembled Mr. Worthington sitting inside with its hat pulled down and pipe jutting. A photographer from a local paper even came out and took a picture of it, saying it would make a good story, but Mr. Morris Worthington came along just as the pictures were being taken. He threatened the paper with "certain actions that would be taken up by his attorney." The photographer went red, then white and could hardly control himself when Worthington jabbed his pipe at the man's chest, as though to dot a period at the end of a sentence. Then he turned, pulled his hat low and stuck the smoldering pipe in his mouth, puffed a couple of smoky puffs, and walked away. So similar was the scarecrow to the original, the newspaperman shook his head and sniggered.

Chapter 4 - Sarah

Bea yelled up to me, "Hey, Hon, you want a soda?"

I was torn from my Grandmother's early world, totally engrossed in her diary. I realized I was falling behind on my sorting. "Not yet, Ma, in a little while though."

I set the diary on the dresser planning to bring it back to Bea's with me tonight and flip through it when I had more time.

That drawer finished up the vanity. I had taken the drawers out and shook them upside down onto the floor, planning to vacuum up any remaining dust and debris that was in them. As I turned this drawer over, I found what seemed like a false bottom. While the thin wood veneer didn't cover the object inside, it did hold it in place so that anyone opening and closing the drawer normally wouldn't notice there was anything concealed there. It was another book, similar in size to Rebecca's diary, worn, but with a nicer, cloth cover. I pulled it out and on opening it, found the words: Private Property of Doris Biracree.

Great, more reading, and it might be kind of saucy if it was hidden under the drawer. I imagined it could make for some fun reading. Since Aunt Doris was dead, and had no relatives, I didn't think it would be much of an invasion of privacy if I read it. After all, probably anyone mentioned in it would be long gone by now. I wondered if it would be as interesting as Rebecca's and put it in the pile to go back with me tonight.

I checked all around the room and everything seemed to be done, all drawers emptied and sorted into piles either for Bea, or me, the shelter, the dump or the auction. The bed was stripped and showed stains and wear and two slight indentations where two people had spent many years sleeping together. The drapes were not worth saving, but it would probably be best if they were left until the house was sold.

I started packing the boxes and carrying them down and putting them in their respective piles at the bottom of the stairs.

By the time I had most of the boxes down from Rebecca's room, I was starting to wane. "What do you say, Bea? Want to pack it in?" I poked my head into Pete's old room.

"I suppose. You know, I don't think they ever touched this room after Pete died. It's clean, no dust, no dirt, but all his old stuff is still here: his clothes, his hat, his wallet, the box where he kept his change, his hairbrush. Everything. Don't you think it's odd? I remember this old wool buffalo-plaid shirt from when I was a kid." She pointed at the heavy black and red checked shirt hanging from the hook on the inside of the closet door. She grabbed the shirt and went to throw it into one of the boxes she had near the door.

"Ma, I think I'd like to have that, ok?"

"Sure, I bet it's warm. Too bad the elbows are worn through, but you can patch them. It's kinda big for you though, don't you think? I suppose you can roll up the sleeves. Just don't wear it out in public."

"Come on, Ma. Let it go."

Bea ignored me, "Well, with just a little sorting we can wrap it up for this room, too."

We decided to go to the pizza place out on the main drag about four miles away. I followed her in my car. It was popular and packed, so we parked on the roadside.

"Want to stay in your old room?" Bea had three bedrooms, one was hers, one was a guest room and one was a catch-all and project room with a bed in it. So I had choices. My old room had been the one turned into the project room when I moved out, since after I moved out she'd spent some time and money redecorating the guest room.

"Nah, I'd like the guest room if you don't mind." I thought it would feel weird to go back to a room that wasn't mine anymore and it changed so much.

"Okay. We've got to go down to the funeral home tomorrow for the service." Bea was very matter of fact. "I thought we could have the memorial service in the evening, that would give people most of the day to get stuff done."

"Sounds good to me, I have almost two weeks off. I told them at work that I needed to come down and help you out here, and they had no problem with it, so whatever you want to do will be fine with me." I saw the mechanic come in and sit in a booth near the door. She greeted the woman who had been waiting for her there, sat down and looked at the menu.

Bea went on, in a matter of fact tone, "I thought we could just have a little service, a couple of flower arrangements, some framed pictures. The funeral director said he would try to get someone like a clergyman to say a few words. Simple, nothing elaborate, I don't expect a big turnout, most of her friends are gone."

"Sounds good," I replied. Bea paid, and we got up to go.

As we left, I smiled at the mechanic who raised her hand hello, while her booth mate stared sourly at me.

Chapter 5 – Sarah

Bea shook the bed gently until I groaned and rolled over.

"Geeze, what bus hit me last night?"

We had sat around Bea's kitchen, drinking martinis until the wee hours the night before. I was surprised at how well she made martinis and how much fun it was to talk to her when we no longer had the issues of adolescence, like puberty, drinking and grades to deal with.

I was getting all the gossip: family, neighborhood and town. Not that our immediate family was all that big. My father had skipped town when I was six and Bea never remarried. Since I was an only child, the only family we had left was a couple of uncles and cousins on Rebecca's side. Rebecca's sister, Gertrude had a couple of boys who had kids so I got to hear about how well they had all done; except for one who was, as Bea put it "a good-for-nothing pothead and drunk," and had even gotten involved with some small time larceny to fund his habits. I expected we might see some of them tonight, except for the ones who would have to travel a long distance.

"Come on down and have a cup of coffee, Honey, that'll perk you right up," Bea said cheerfully as she moved through the room folding the clothes I'd dropped onto the chair and straightening the throw rug with her foot.

The smell of the coffee almost made me gag, but splashing some cold water on my face and running a comb through my hair helped. Then, while appraising myself in the mirror, I thought, well, I don't look too bad for someone in her mid thirties after a 3-martini night.

Thankfully, Bea didn't start cooking the eggs until I had gotten well into my second cup of coffee and by then, as Bea had predicted, I did start to feel better.

Bea's kitchen, like the rest of her house, bordered on the modern style. I supposed it was a rebellious part of her that didn't want to be like her mother and grandmother with all the lace doilies and Victorian fringed lamp shades. It wasn't a spare kitchen or cold like some modern furnishings, but it had clean lines and no frilly stuff. Like Bea, it was no nonsense and utilitarian.

Bea was a practical woman who rarely let her emotions rule. She'd seen enough of life not to expect the fairytale ending and when my father left, she had already been working as an accountant so it was hardly a bump in the road of her life. When I was a kid, and got out of school in the afternoon, I would go next door to Cheryl's and have juice and cookies and play with Cheryl's son Jeff. Cheryl was Bea's best friend, and would go out of her way to pick me up or take me in when Bea was late at work. Bea and I made our way through life, sometimes with peanut butter and jelly, once in a great while with steak.

"How's Cheryl?" I asked since I hadn't heard Bea talk about her in a while.

"Hmph," Bea snorted, "We had a falling out. I haven't talked to her in over a year."

"Really? Wow. You guys used to be inseparable." I was truly surprised, remembering all the evenings around our kitchen table or Cheryl's, playing cards or a board game, Cheryl inhaling Marlboro smoke through her nose, which I thought was very cool, and Mom with a cold Bud; all of us laughing until I was out of breath.

"What happened?"

"I don't want to talk about it right now, ok?" Bea put the pan roughly into the sink to signal that the discussion was over.

I walked over to the window and looked across the side yard to Cheryl's house.

"She moved away. Last year." Bea's answer was matter of fact, but her tone said: don't ask me anything more. I was certainly curious, but I knew better than to press her. I suspected that with time and perhaps a few martinis she might tell me.

I think that no matter how old you are, there is something strange and comforting about staying overnight in your childhood home. Strange because of all the memories and how you see them now from the perspective of adulthood. Comforting because if you were lucky enough to have a safe childhood home, that security and warmth envelopes you. It would always be a safe place, somewhere that you could escape to when the rest of the world seemed too insane or dangerous. That is, of course, if you were lucky enough to have a safe and sane home. Once I left home and joined the "real world," I found that there were not many of us that had that benefit. Many were safe, but many had varying degrees of insanity, ranging from slightly quirky to totally nuts. The ones that weren't safe often had a predatory parent who had a penchant for physical or sexual abuse. I was surprised how common this was, since my family life was fairly ordinary by most standards.

Other than having my father leave, my life was fairly run-of-the mill. I don't remember much before he left, only that they fought a lot. Bea was busy trying to keep us clothed, fed and with a roof over our heads while working full time. I was busy trying to get passing grades. Much of her younger life is shrouded in mystery to me, as she rarely talked about it and seemed to give only standard or superficial answers to probing or leading questions. If there was dysfunction there, she didn't wear it on her sleeve. I wanted to hear more about her younger life, especially after seeing Rebecca's journal and maybe, when I had time to read Aunt Doris's, it would reveal even more of what kind of home Bea was born into. I was hoping too, that this week with her would make our sometimes rocky relationship easier, and that she would open up. Certainly I was no prize during my teenage years, but with that behind us, well, who knows?

I put the breakfast dishes into the dishwasher and went to put together my outfit for our evening at the funeral home.

Chapter 6 – Sarah

We arrived at the funeral home early so we could do a viewing before anyone else arrived. Since we only expected a small gathering, the funeral director led us into one of the smaller rooms Bea had selected.

She had chosen a modest casket for Rebecca, and when we were led in, the lights were low, several flower arrangements had been tastefully placed, and subdued music was being piped in. It was a production; the rows of chairs facing the casket, several overstuffed chairs up in the front, a torchier on each end of the casket, everything placed to lead the eye to the casket and the small, still figure within. Rebecca looked good, as though she were sleeping, but not quite natural. Something was just a bit off. It's odd to see people you've known in life and then to see them laid out in a casket. Usually they look good, everyone says so, but they don't look quite right. They don't look like the sleeping versions of themselves, something looks awry.

Rebecca had started out as a small person, but as she aged she became shorter and shorter. In the casket, sunken down on the satin pillow, she was downright tiny. Her white curls were done up fancier than she ever would have had them, and with mascara defining her eyelashes and blush on her pale cheeks, it was Grandma, and yet not quite. All pretty unusual for a woman who preferred flour on her face and garden dirt under her fingernails.

In the pictures I'd seen of her as a younger woman, she looked lady-like and rather attractive for her time, probably pretty fashionable. But as a grandmother and housewife, the daily toil took all of the time she could muster and looking fancy wasn't one of her top priorities.

Bea put a couple of framed pictures of her mother out on the reception table. One showed Rebecca and Pete and Doris, Pete in the middle with his arms on both their shoulders. In it, they were all smiling and looking rather devilish. She put another out that I barely recognized until I studied it for a minute. It was of Becky and Doris when they were very young, each with their arm on the other's shoulder, wearing long white bibbed aprons with white sleeve coverings and long skirts.

I took the time to look through these pictures. I'd never seen the one of Becky and Doris before; it looked like they had just stopped some busy task long enough for someone to photograph them, impromptu, hair up but with some strands hanging loose. It was like another glimpse through a window into Becky's youth. I felt I was there for a brief moment, that I existed in her time, in her world.

As I was holding this picture, the funeral director came in and walked with Bea over to Rebecca's casket. They were talking in low voices as I went over to join them. Bea stood with her hand on the edge, "Give it to Sarah. I'm sure she would want it," she said and both of them turned to me. The funeral director pulled a handkerchief out of his pocket, unfolded it and handed the small gold wedding band enfolded within to me. "Is this Rebecca's?" I said looking from him to Bea. They both nodded that it was. I was confused, thinking that it was odd, that there was already one at her home, in the box I had found. I tried this ring on. It didn't fit my ring finger, but did fit my pinky.

Just as I was going to take it off to see if there was anything inscribed inside, Uncle Russell and my cousin Jake walked in. Russell went over to hug Bea, and Jake came and put his arms around me. Uncle Russell disengaged from Bea and came over and hugged me. I hadn't seen them in several years so was surprised to see how much each had aged. Russell and Bea started to make small talk about how good Rebecca looked. Jake said he needed a cigarette, and asked if I would like to go outside with him.

"Geeze, I hate these things," he said exhaling the smoke. We stood out on the front porch of the funeral home stepping aside for other people to enter. There was a second memorial service tonight and it seemed that person was having a number of visitors.

"You're looking good; the city life must agree with you." He smiled his charming smile. "Someone as attractive as you should have been snatched up years ago. Are you still seeing that same guy, what was he, a salesman? Why hasn't he popped the question yet?" Not giving me time to answer the first question, he ran one into the other, and then started to talk about himself and his successful law practice. This was fine with me. I would just as well listen or at least look like I was listening, than to explain my personal life to someone whom I wouldn't see until the next funeral. As he talked about himself, his wife, his partners at the law practice, on and on, I started to think about the ring, as I rolled it around and around on my pinkie.

Several people came for the other wake and then people from town that I knew. I excused myself and went in to be with Bea, not wanting to leave her standing there alone. When I went in, she sat down in one of the big comfortable chairs up front, and I sat in the one next to her. "I arranged to have someone come and say a few words. Since she hasn't been to church in years, it's hard to get a priest to come out." She reached over and patted my hand.

A few people were sitting, scattered, in the folding chairs in the back. Several more arrived, walked over to the casket, knelt, looked like they were saying a little prayer, crossed themselves and came over. Bea and I rose to greet them.

More people came, seemingly all with the same condolences, and we with the same thank you. The same thoughts were repeated over and over. "Thankfully, she didn't suffer long," or "She had a good, long life."

A few relatives trooped through, and in the receiving line, Bea introduced me to Mike, Rebecca's neighbor and his son, Harry. Mike had an oddly familiar face; I wasn't sure if I'd met him before, maybe when I was a kid. Harry was pleasant and seemed the opposite of my cousin Jake, quiet and unassuming with intense eyes. Mike was serious and reserved. Next were some of Bea's old co-workers and neighbors, some neighbors of Rebecca's, even the mechanic who fixed my flat a few days before.

She shook Bea's hand and said how sorry she was, and then mentioned she had worked on Rebecca's old Chevy over the years. She said it was in really good shape, and if we needed to get rid of it she would help. She smiled at me, took my hand, said she was sorry for my loss and that she really liked Rebecca and Doris and would miss them. Then she walked to the back of the room, and sat next to several others talking quietly.

Small towns, that's all I could think, small towns with lots of characters and secrets.

Chapter 7 – Sarah

We were emotionally drained when we got home, but Bea asked me if I wanted some sherry, and I said it sounded good. We settled into the deep couch in the small, eclectic living room and she poured a liberal glass of sherry for each of us. We relaxed there, the lamp next to the sofa giving off a soft warm glow. She sipped the sherry, sat back, put her feet up, closed her eyes, and gave a good long sigh. She hadn't shed a tear, said she just wasn't ready, that she felt guilty about it, but the tears just wouldn't come.

We talked about the family, how Uncle Russell and his wife were doing and how very well Jake was doing, even though she heard he was starting to attend a few too many cocktail parties. She gossiped some more about the neighbors and the old friends from work. It was true, as we got older, we only saw people and caught up with them at funerals and weddings, and now it seemed that it was mostly funerals. She talked a little about Mike and Harry, and how when she was really young they were friendly, but somehow the families grew apart.

"Harry seems like a nice guy, we should invite him over." She dropped it casually, giving me a sideways glance. I didn't respond, but thought to myself that he did seem nice.

We talked about my childhood, and even talked a little about hers. She fixed us a plate of cheese and crackers and more sherry. We must have stayed up until 2 a.m. And even though I wasn't married or engaged and didn't even have anyone serious in the wings, she didn't land on the subject tonight. It was a night just for us, for us and Rebecca. She talked about how good Rebecca could cook, and how funny she was at times making jokes about her failing eyesight and hearing and peeing her pants, when she sneezed. How much Bea loved the vacations they took in their station wagon to the Adirondacks.

"It was sudden." Bea reflected, "She almost made it to her birthday. Remember, she was excited about us taking her out to dinner. Now you're here and instead of dinner, we're having her funeral. I had no idea; I thought she was doing pretty well on her own without Doris. The doctor said it was her heart. I found her when I came over to pick her up to go shopping for her birthday dinner outfit. I called and there was no answer, and when I got to the house, the door was locked and it was dark inside. That was unusual right there. I started to feel alarmed. I sort of knew something was wrong. I unlocked the door and called, but no answer. I looked around and then went upstairs and she was in bed. I don't think she ever woke up, just passed peacefully in her sleep. I'll miss her; she was a ticket."

Finally, we had a last toast to Rebecca and with the warm haze of sherry on us, we both found our eyes welling up for the little old white haired lady that was her mother and my grandmother.

When I settled into bed and turned the light out, my hand went to the ring and I turned it around a few more times. I sat up and turned the light back on, took the ring off and squinted to see if there was writing on the inside. "*From DB To RM With All My Love,*" I dropped it on the blanket. I picked it up.

From DB to RM. DB to RM … DB to RM? Doris Biracree to Rebecca Moorhouse? Doris and Rebecca? My Grandmother and her housekeeper? This must be some kind of mistake … someone else's initials, or what? … A joke? Wait, no, not a joke, a friendship ring? I got up and found the ring box. I'd left it on the guest room dresser, having forgotten to give it to Bea.

I opened the box, took out the ring and put my glasses on this time. "*RM to DB, Love of My Life*". I just didn't understand. What does this mean? There must be a mistake. They must have been the best of friends. The rings were identical, simple wedding bands, no filigree, nor other markings. Wedding bands … wedding bands … I mused.

This was just too confusing for me. I was exhausted, but I couldn't sleep. I put Rebecca's ring back on. I lay back down hoping for sleep, hoping to make sense of this. Bea would be able to explain this, there's got to be some simple explanation. They had been the best of friends, and it was obvious from that picture at the funeral home. They had some kind of childhood pact, some kind of special relationship.

I wanted to sleep, but couldn't. Bea would now be totally asleep after the sherry. I didn't want to wake her now for something so silly, just to put my mind at ease for something that would be easily explained away.

Then I remembered the journal, "Private Property of Doris Biracree". It was sitting along with a few other treasures on the dresser with the ring box. Well that might just explain it all, I decided. At least I could fall asleep reading, if nothing else. I climbed back into bed and opened the "Private Property of Doris Biracree".

Chapter 8 – Doris

Friday – Sept. 9, 1898

I'm heading off to make my fortune tomorrow. I think the farm is sustaining itself, but I don't think I will ever get anywhere if I don't try to become more independent. Papa won't leave the farm to me and I don't want to work as hard as Mama does. She works from sunrise to sunset and beyond. She never, ever stops. I know I'm not ready to be somebody's wife yet, so, my adventure begins. Cousin Horace said that there is work at the mill where he is a mechanic; they need help and are hiring. A man came through town a couple of weeks ago to sign up girls to work at the mill. He convinced several other families that mill work is safe. The girls are well fed, respectable, and they are not allowed to stay out late or drink and they are expected to go to church on Sunday. The girls stay together in a boarding house close to the mill, and are watched over by a house matron.

I begged Papa and he agreed. I think he understands that there is a restless part of me that yearns for a life beyond the farm. Papa told Mama, who cried for a while, but with all the work she had to do she couldn't indulge in such sadness for long. He had to persuade Ma because she didn't want me to go. It would be one less pair of hands to help out, and she would miss me, too. I joked with her and told her I could send some money home, and I could come back home for the summer to help at the farm and then bring her a nice present.

Even though I'm excited about going on this adventure, I'm scared too. What if I'm not strong enough, or fast enough? What if I don't learn quickly enough, will they send me back home? Will I owe the mill for that training and the boarding house for staying there? What if I become sick and can't work? What will happen to me then?

My little sister came in to hug me and climbed into bed next to me while I am writing this. I will miss her, little Abigail. I just kissed her on the top of her dear little head. She has snuggled up under my arm and I have no doubts she will shortly be asleep.

We had a beautiful apple pie tonight, made special with the early apples. Ma said it was for my send off and then Pa gave me eight silver dollars telling me to be careful with them, and that they would tide me over until I could start collecting my pay.

I packed up several of my good dresses and bonnets into a bandbox and Ma slipped me a pair of wool mittens she'd just knitted and a new handkerchief. I feel luckier than anyone I know to have such a good family.

I went out and did the chores with Abby and Jared this evening and picked some of the summer squash for supper. The winter squash isn't quite ready yet and I won't be here to help

harvest it and store it away in the cellar. I was able to get a couple bushel of potatoes dug. They should be dry enough by tomorrow to put down.

I was really busy today trying to help as much as I could before I left – probably did more work today than I normally do in two, trying so hard to make Ma happy.

I will make them proud when I get to the mill. I can be self-sufficient and independent and help out a little with payments back home here, too. As I packed, I tucked my little picture of Mom and Abigail into the folds of my favorite shawl. I feel ready for anything now.

Sat. Sept. 10, 1898

I've arrived in Willimantic! The trip was long but not too tiring. I have just been settled into my room at the Elms Boarding House. The matron left me to put my belongings away. I have a small dresser where I have put my personal items and several hooks where I have hung my dresses and coat. I find I can keep my book and writing paper in my bandbox under the bed, so it is easy to take out and write on. And if I sit on the edge of the bed, I can look out the window and see the mill where I soon will be starting to work. It is a long three-story stone building, with rows of tall windows all along the sides. It is, I am sure, the largest building I have ever seen, awesome and forbidding and business-like, with a tower and large doors and an iron fence all around. Bells ring, and as I watch, troupes of women walk in ones and twos towards the boarding house. Other men and women go out the gate and turn down the street towards the rows of homes that I can see if I lean to the side. These are rows of look-alike houses with two front doors, wisps of smoke come from the chimneys. I must go down to supper shortly where I will meet many of the other mill girls. Although nervous and excited, I miss Mama and Pa and Abby.

Sun. Sept. 11, 1898

We were woken early to go to the church. It is a Presbyterian which I am not a member of, but we are required to attend this by the mill rules.

I was shown the list of rules by the Matron of this house, who seems nice enough, and who also gave me a written copy of them. The rules are many and strict. No drinking. No smoking. We must be in the house by 10 p.m. or we will be locked out, unless of course we have a valid reason. We must regularly attend the church, and pay pew fees from our salary. The room and board here at the house will also be taken from our salary as will the cost of our working ensembles. Our work days are run by bells: Bells to wake us, bells to start work, bells to go to breakfast, bells for dinner, bells for supper and so on. If we're late at the mill for our first bell to start work, or the bell to return from dinner, we're locked out and our pay is docked. It is all very structured, but it doesn't seem much harder than waking for school or morning chores. The company requires that we sign a statement saying we agree to abide by the rules. If one follows the rules, they are rewarded with room, board, and a pay envelope full of money that is all theirs – what riches!

I will be starting tomorrow as an alternate, which means that I won't have a full time operative position until one opens up and I have gotten enough experience.

Tues. Sept. 13, 1898

The first day was exhausting, but I have managed through it and another. Oh, how my feet do hurt. I have taken the time to write several letters which makes my time at my precious book short, but I will be sure to write more tomorrow.

Wed. Sept. 14, 1898

I am more tired today than yesterday; I cannot stay awake to write letters and to write to you, my dear book. How I miss Mama and Abigail. Though the food is good and of adequate quantity, the time that we have for breakfast and dinner is not enough to eat leisurely. I am learning to gulp it down quickly like the other girls before the bell rings to call us back to the mill. Fortunately, the mill is nearby and we can all file down to it in rapid procession.

I had hoped my roommate would be a likeable sort, but am finding her to be rather inconsiderate. I'm writing now in the common room as it is more comfortable than writing on the bandbox in our room.

Thurs. Sept. 15, 1898

I've gotten my work ensemble, a large white apron with good pockets, a set of compact scissors for trimming errant threads and cleaning up after spliced threads, and arm covers to protect my blouse sleeves. I've been shown how to tuck the scissors into the apron waistband so that they are readily available. I find I must keep my hair up or pulled back, so that it won't get caught in the machinery. I don't have enough hair pins to do this effectively, and hope to purchase a packet once I am paid. We leave our aprons at the mill in the changing room and they are laundered for us weekly. The mill so far is surprisingly warm although the days have not yet gotten cold. The air is moist and full of dust. I'm told the plants lining some of the walls are kept and watered liberally to keep the moisture in the air. The sound of the machines is deafening and it would be impossible to talk normally above it even if we were allowed. One of the girls has pasted up a poem on a nearby window and another girl has pasted a picture, their diversions from the day-to-day drudgery.

Sat. Sept. 17, 1898

Oh, I must say that my feet are sore today. I am still working at the temporary position, but my teacher is encouraging, and tells me I am learn-ing quickly and I should expect to become a full fledged operative within the next month. I am working now at the carding machines, but it may be possible to move to spinning soon. There are all sorts of women here and of all ages. Some are my own age, but many are older, and some are very young, perhaps no more than ten. All of us are diligent and want to give the mill our best work. We are proud of our product. We got out early today, 1 o'clock, and do not need to return to work until Monday at 6 a.m. I hope to take some of the money Papa gave me and purchase that packet of pins for my hair, and maybe a new ribbon. I don't feel as tired today and may try to write a letter to Abigail and Mama. I wish I could find a private spot to write. It's not as comfortable as I had imagined trying to write in my room.

I never know when my roommate will come in and stomp around and look sullen, but there is no privacy anywhere else. It is proving to be the darkest side of my new surroundings.

Sun. Sept. 18, 1898

My roommate has thrown my clothes onto the floor, saying that the hook I had been using was hers and I shouldn't be using it. She threatened to cut my clothes up if I complained. I am sorely distressed over this as we are thrown into such close proximity, but I sleep far to my side of the bed, and she moves about and takes more space. I folded my dresses and placed them on my small dresser. I am still hoping that once we have gotten more well acquainted, she will be kinder to me.

I'm not fond of the Presbyterian Church which we attended this morning. The service is so different from our little congregation back home. I am willing to attend, as this is where we all troupe down together and I can meet some of the other girls. They are mostly very pleasant and tidy, and some have offered to help me sew a new pattern dress. I have survived my first week.

Chapter 9 - Sarah

When I woke, Bea was gone; she had left long before I got up. On the kitchen table next to a bowl there was a note saying she had to go down to the lawyers and sign some papers, and that I should try the new cereal she left on the counter.

I was disappointed to find her gone. So much was going through my mind. The rings. Aunt Doris's journal. I was interested in reading about Doris starting out her young work life at the mill. I poured myself a cup of good, dark, coffee and took it upstairs. I took the ring from the box and inspected it in the sunlight. Clean, cool and golden, no question as to the initials, the outside was worn and scratched, but the inside was polished smooth as glass. I took the other ring off, it was in the same condition, with a slightly different sentiment and the initials were transposed.

Bea would know, she would understand. I was sure of it. Theirs must have been a close friendship of many years, perhaps 60 or more, maybe even before Pete married Rebecca. No other possibility was even within the realm of my imagination, unthinkable. To imagine my Grandmother might be a homosexual, well, that is just impossible, and somehow frightening.

I pulled on my jeans and decided to go out for breakfast, packing the journal into my bag, along with my wallet and the keys to Rebecca's house. Then I went back and left a note for Bea.

The breakfast at the little diner was abundant and greasy and satisfying. I rarely have bacon and eggs, but today it seemed like the thing to do, and I topped it off with rye toast, butter and more black coffee. It was a decadent meal, for sure.

As I ate and read the paper, I found my mind wandering to the events of the last few days: the funeral home, my egocentric cousin, the neighbor's son, the mechanic, the rings and journals, and Rebecca and Doris, who I now feel as if I have always known and yet never known, but that, I imagined, would soon change as I dive into the diaries. It was wishful thinking on my part, but it would have been nice to read their journals before they were gone, and ask them about their lives and jobs and family.

I was lucky to have Bea, who seems to have mellowed even in just the last week. I didn't have a husband or even a special boyfriend, but I wasn't lonely. I liked the people at work, and had some very good friends, the kind of friends who see you through hard times and don't complain when you do the same stupid, doomed-to-fail relationship thing over and over. Death brings a tumbling and jumbling of thoughts so that even one's daily events are viewed and inspected from many different perspectives.

One of Rebecca's neighbors came in, I recognized her from the wake. She saw me and waved and made her way over to my booth.

"Hi there Honey, how are you doing?" she said in a New England nasal twang.

"OK, I'm doing OK."

"Well, that was a nice ceremony you and your mom had for Rebecca, we sure will miss her. She was a real sweetie."

"Yeah, I'll miss her too. Did you see much of her?"

"Oh yes, she was out puttering in the yard all the time. And she and Doris would often be out walking on the road, arm in arm. They loved walking the old road, never got tired of it, almost every day. When they passed by the house, they often paused and had a story about something down the road, a flock of turkeys, or some deer or just the birds singing. Rebecca was so sweet, Doris too, yes, we certainly will miss them."

As she was talking and patting my hand, a few people came into the diner. One sat at the counter, the other, the mechanic, came over to my booth. Rebecca's neighbor pulled her hand back and frowned ever so slightly.

"Well, I just came in to pick up a sandwich for Carl, good to see you, dear, you take care, and if you need anything, you just come on over." She said this as she was walking away.

The mechanic sat down in my booth across from me.

"Hi, how's the tire?" She smiled.

I liked her smile, it was open and warm and real.

"The car and the tire are just fine, thanks to you. I'm sorry, but I don't remember your name."

"Alice, my name is Alice Rittenmeyer. I live near the center, not far from the garage. That makes it really convenient for me to go out on some of those late night calls that sometimes come in – that's one reason that Ralph likes me so much." She turned and called to a waitress. "Hey, can I get a coffee over here?" She turned back to me, "You don't mind if I sit with you for a minute? I'm just taking a little break and happened to see your car out front and hoped you wouldn't mind…"

"No, no that's fine."

"So, are you cleaning out your Grandma's old place?"

"Yes, but it's not too bad. They don't seem to have been serious pack rats."

"Boy, lucky you, my mother is such a collector. I'm always afraid she'll have a fire and the escape routes will be blocked with stuff she's been collecting. It's not anything good, but somehow she can't part with any of it. You know what I mean? Old magazines, jars, used envelopes, plastic bags, all kinds of stuff. Stuff that could and should be, tossed out. Geeze, I sure hope I don't get like that. Maybe it has something to do with living through the depression. Are you ever afraid of becoming your mother?" She was a real live wire, and asked so many questions I didn't know where to start.

"Yeah, sometimes I worry about becoming like my mother, but lately, my mother has been a real champ, not bugging me too much about boyfriends, or children or my job or much of anything. I'm thinking Rebecca's passing has had a bigger impact than she's able to admit."

"I know what you mean. When my grandmother died, my mother tried to go along like it didn't bother her, not totally in denial, but, you know, not really mourning. It was like she was sort of in shock. Then, a couple months later, she found an old card her mom had sent, and she broke down. She just cried and cried." Alice looked up at the clock. "Geeze, I gotta go, I was only gonna stop in for a minute. Good to see you again…"

"Sarah." I put my hand out and Alice shook it.

"How long are you going to be around, Sarah?" She said as she rose to go to the register.

"I was planning to go back this next weekend, but I may stay a little longer. I have enough vacation and I don't think my boss would mind." The decision was made as I said it; I hadn't even thought about taking more time.

"Great, maybe we can get together for a drink or a movie or something." She hesitated long enough for me to nod yes, then smiled and waved as she headed out the door. I smiled and waved back.

Chapter 10 – Doris

Mon. Sept. 19, 1898

I am back at the mill working today, long hours, but I am looking forward to my first payday this Saturday.

My teacher and helper, Susan, is giving me directions as to what will align me for an operative position. Of course I have heard it all, but I appreciate that she stresses the value that the mill bosses place on morally upright and diligent girls. The company feels that these girls are the ones who will make the best quality product. Bad girls, she says, don't care as much and they will be more careless with the threads. They cost the company more because they let mistakes go through that will then need to be repaired by someone else. She's also been telling me who to watch out for, as they are not only troublemakers, but also whose position I may aspire to if they continue to be late. The mill bosses don't tolerate tardiness and will soon find a ready pair of hands to take over for those who don't have a suitable interest in their work. We talk about these things on our march to breakfast and lunch and back. Susan is in our house, but on the first floor. The longer you have been in the house, the better choice of rooms you get. The first floor is favored and closer to the boiler in the winter. I asked her about my roommate, hoping she could tell me that she was one of the bad girls who would soon be replaced, but she did not know of her.

Tues. Sept. 20, 1898

The girls were all excited when the new young machinist walked through to work on a winder. Their eyes went from one to the other, all giving small signals with their hands so that all of them looked at him as he went down the rows of machines. Some of them put the backs of their hands to their mouths and made as to giggle behind them, some others colored and looked away. He was a handsome fellow, but I thought the girls were being silly.

Several of us who work on the same floor sat together in the parlor tonight playing a game of Parcheesi and our talk eventually went to the machinist. When one of them asked me what I thought, I told her that he held no interest for me as I wasn't ready to think about marrying. You can still have an opinion, another said. And I told her that I thought he would make someone a good husband someday, but not my husband. Everyone stopped for a second and looked at me. Esther, a new friend, giggled nervously; but I just continued to play the game, which resumed shortly. Why is it so strange that a woman who has just gained financial independence would also want her freedom?

Wed. Sept. 21, 1898

My dear book, I am too tired to write much this evening. The long days are wearing on me. I will try to get abed earlier tonight and so be more refreshed tomorrow. That way I may also be able to avoid any unpleasantness with my roommate.

Thurs. Sept. 22 1898

Dear book, I must write this in haste as I expect my roommate to return soon. Last evening, as I retired early, my roommate arrived after me, and began to say mean things. She pushed my dresses off of the dresser where I had folded and laid them when she took them from the wall hooks. I got up and picked up each dress and folded it and started to again put it on the dresser. I asked her why she was being so cruel to me, as I did her no harm.

She came at me as though to hit me, but I grabbed her arm and she stopped and gave me an anguished look, and then began to cry, and cried very hard. I hugged her as she sobbed out that her previous roommate had left with the pleurisy, and was not coming back and that she missed her profoundly. She said that she was afraid to get close to a new roommate, fearing another loss. Rebecca, I said, as I petted her hair, it's all right, I will be your roommate now if you will have me, and she hugged me tighter, and I held her until she was subdued.

I expect she will be in soon, and I am hoping we will still be on the friendlier terms we were yesterday.

Chapter 11 – Sarah

I rattled around Rebecca's home, trying to focus on the next steps in the process of emptying the home out. As I wandered from room to room, picking up bits of paper and soda cans and consolidating the trash, I was struck by how comfortable the old house was. As it became emptier, the soundness and structural beauty shone through. The columns between the living room and the middle parlor were still the varnished dark oak that no one had yet had a chance to paint over or remove. Rebecca had proudly displayed her china in the built-in oak corner cabinet. Then there was that beautiful, heavy oak banister leading up the stairs. The wood trimmed windows overlooked the lawn and flower garden. It was a warm and inviting home. For the first time, I wondered how far into the real estate process Bea had gotten. Did she have a realtor or interested party? It must be hard to part with your past, to drive by your childhood home where someone else is now living, where they are cutting down trees that you once cherished and pulling up flowers you planted with care. It's strange to lose that solid part of your past, and have the past become only memories. It's an odd twist of reality, when an old home is gone and a carwash put up in its place; or a barn removed or an ancient tree cut down – in your mind's eye, they still exist, like that phantom pain of a lost limb. If I owned and lived at the house, Bea would be spared that, and as much as she seems unemotional about her past and homestead, I'm sure she'd like to see it stay in the family.

I went into the basement and checked out the furnace, which was a large old boiler packed in some kind of plaster insulation. The old radiators upstairs really seemed to put out the heat, so no problem there. There was some old, cloth covered wiring and a few old push button switches. But there also was a new panel with new wiring. I could see that someone was trying to keep pace with the times and have it upgraded. Several of the windows upstairs had been replaced, too, with more efficient ones.

Where was I going with all this? Did I want to buy this old house? I didn't have a house, but I did have an apartment, and a good job. Well, I guess this could be an investment. I was thinking about it, thinking about buying my grandparent's home. I hadn't taken leave of my senses, but it was pretty drastic and, well, unexpected. No matter what, I thought, it didn't hurt to look. I wandered around some more, went upstairs, into Rebecca's room once more, opening the closet. Then I entered Doris's room, it was smaller, with a little closet, but still with a nice view out over the back garden with the lilac bush and the bench. We still needed to go through all her stuff, but like Rebecca's room, it didn't look that cluttered.

The bathroom had its pluses and minuses. It was large, but the fixtures were old. I liked the claw-foot tub and pedestal sink, but the toilet was just too old and would have to be replaced, someday.

The attic, which you got to from a small door off the second floor landing, was larger than I expected, with slanted ceilings and lath that had horsehair and plaster oozing from it. A couple of small windows gave enough light so that you could not only see, but also could imagine a little artists loft up there. Several straight-backed chairs, a couple of boxes, a suitcase and a hatbox were sitting at the top of the stairs. I carried them all down to the second floor landing. Sometimes the rummaging was fun, finding all this old stuff, sort of like a treasure hunt. I decided to take all of the boxes to Bea's with me, and go through them all there.

I wandered in the garden, seeing the potential and yet imagining all the work that would be necessary to bring it back. The old vegetable garden down below would also be easy to rejuvenate with the help of a tiller and some cow manure.

As I loaded the last box from the attic into my car, I could see a car kicking up dust as it wove its way down the dirt road. Bea pulled in and stepped out, dressed in her "Sunday go to meeting" clothes, as she occasionally liked to refer to them.

"So, how was it at the lawyer's?"

"Just the legal stuff, you know, but the world pivots around the lawyers and their schedules."

"Yeah, right. So tell me, what's the status of the house? Do you have a realtor or a buyer?"

Bea turned and gave me a quizzical look. Do mothers always know when something is up?

"No, not yet. I was going to go to the realtor, but hadn't had a chance. Why, are you interested?" OK, Bea had me pegged.

"Well, it crossed my mind. As I was looking around I thought it looked pretty nice; I know it needs some cleaning up, and a few repairs. I'd probably have to replace the boiler someday and some of the wiring. But, if it was reasonable enough, it could be a good investment."

"In-VEST-MENT? She said it as though it were three words. "Are you planning to live in it or rent it out?"

"Actually, I hadn't gotten that far. I was just sort of musing, and it might not amount to anything." I had to be honest with her. "Hey, I'm hungry. I got a late start, a late breakfast, and I missed lunch. Want to go out for dinner? My treat. I have a lot of questions for you, and not just about the house."

Chapter 12 – Doris

Sat. Sept. 24, 1898

Well, I have gotten my first payroll. I am an independent woman. I also have a new friend, Rebecca, my roommate, as unlikely as it might seem. She has become a fun partner in the boarding house and I know we will have some fine adventures together.

This afternoon, after I received my pay, Rebecca and I walked downtown and went to the ladies store to see their goods. Becky was putting payment on a silk and wool shawl she could wear to church and a pair of kid gloves. While we were there, I found the most beautiful comb and brush and mirror set made of ivory. It was quite expensive, but I felt that since this was my first payday, I should get myself something I would remember. So, using almost all that I had left over from the boarding house and pew payment, I walked out with a special treasure. I don't think I can tell Mama just yet, as she would think it a wasteful way to spend my hard earned money, but Rebecca whole-heartedly approved. The set sits now on my little dresser and I am feeling very proud and pleased.

Sun. Sept. 25, 1898

Rebecca and I and a number of others trouped off together to the Presbyterian Church this morning. Then, in the afternoon, a bunch of us went to the Band and Choral Concert at the opera house. They were featuring a famous singer who had a voice like an angel that drifted over the crowd like silk. Everyone hushed when she sang "Barbara Allen" and the conductor gave her a bouquet of flowers when she was finished. I have never heard such a voice. Dear book, if only I could describe it in a way to do it justice. Rebecca sat with me and squeezed my hand when she sang the last song, "Mary Hamilton". I have never heard anything so beautiful before. We all chatted gaily on the walk back. I have never been to such a fine concert before, and I am sure my world cannot get any more enjoyable.

The only dark note was when several girls laughed at my old-fashioned hat, but Rebecca put her arm through mine, her nose up and we walked briskly away. We plan to look for a newer hat that I may be able to get after my next payday.

Mon. Sept. 26, 1898

Alas, back to the work again, but I am being assured that I will get the operative position in the next month. This will bring a substantial raise in salary which will help me to put some savings away. Susan says that I am showing noticeable improvement in my skills and speed and she has brought this up with the overseer.

Wed. Sept. 28, 1898

We are at the company library this evening. It's on the third floor of the mill store and is very close to the mill and to the Elms. It is a beautiful library full of handsome books and two large warm fireplaces. Some of the girls are taught classes here in English and Mathematics. They have a circulating library which brings us new literature and periodicals regularly and the newspapers are delivered daily, even the Bulletin and the Times. The company store and mill offices are on the lower floors and we must pass our paymaster and some of the agent's offices on the way up.

I can write comfortably here with good gas lamps giving me lots of light. Rebecca is across the table, writing letters home. Several of the mill boys are also studying up here and they often try to make conversation and become our friends. I am not interested in that right now. As an independent woman who can pay her own way, I can wait until I feel the time is right and don't even want to be tempted to become friendly.

Thurs. Sept. 29, 1898

Mrs. Dority, our house matron, has told us that a special dessert is planned for Friday supper and not to leave too early for the library or we would miss this treat. Mrs. Dority is a good house matron; she is a good cook and cares for her girls, but sometimes lectures them so that they will not be "led astray" as she says. She says that she came here eight years ago with her three children after her husband died and she couldn't make enough of a living to care for her children just by housekeeping. She heard of this job through an acquaintance, applied immediately and got it. Now her children are grown and she is able to save some money for her older years. Sometimes she sits down with us after the meal as we linger over tea. She tells us of the bad girls, and what they did to get released, and then tells us of the good girls and how they went on to marry well or continue schooling and become teachers. I am learning that many girls do not work at the mill for long periods, perhaps only 2 or 3 years, until they can amass a dowry or help a brother through college or a parent out of debt. Then they move on to marry or to other work with some of them opening their own shops in town sewing clothes or making hats. I am not yet sure what I will do, or how long I will be here, but the thrill of independence is most exciting, and I hope to be thrifty and save carefully.

Fri. Sept. 30, 1898

It was, fortunately, one of those warm days as Mrs. Dority made ice cream for dessert. Well, we actually all helped. We donned aprons and took turns at the crank – Esther sat next to me and tried to steady the wooden barrel as I cranked. It was wonderful and we all scooped it into our bowls from the barrel until finally there was none left. She had borrowed the ice cream maker from one of the other houses and we made good use of it before she had to return it.

Sat. Oct 1, 1898

I am getting comfortable here. I'm making good friends and don't feel as homesick as I did when I first arrived. The long, busy days with the regular bells and work that is not too difficult bring a certain steadiness to our lives. After we got out of work today, Rebecca and I strolled around town, admiring the beautiful dresses in the shop windows and the new shoes and hats. We stopped at the Italian market with all the fruits piled high in boxes out front, and bought ourselves a little bag of Italian sweets which tasted of anise and almonds. As we walked arm in arm home Becky talked with an Italian accent and we laughed until we cried. "Dry dees leetle zugars," she'd say and we'd start laughing again. I am so happy here.

Sun. Oct. 2, 1898

After church today we joined a number of other girls in a wagon that was going out to a farm to pick apples. We picked enough so that our Boarding House would have 10 bushels. The Boarding House paid for them, but we would get the benefit of many apple desserts. Now my arms are sore from holding them over my head in an unnatural position for so long.

Chapter 13 – Sarah

Bea knew of a nice restaurant on the main drag about five miles away from her home. We got a comfortable booth and ordered wine and appetizers. Once the wine came, and we had a few sips and looked around at the other diners, I took the ring off and handed it to Bea. "This is Rebecca's. It's the ring the funeral director gave to me. Read the inscription."

Bea put her glasses on and squinted at the tiny writing, moving it around until she could get the best light, "From DB To RM With All My Love". She read it out loud slowly as though she was having trouble making it out. Bea got a faraway look, as though she was remembering something, or working out something in her mind. Then her gaze focused and flashed to me.

"You got this the other night at the funeral parlor?"

"Yes, and there is another that I found in Rebecca's room, not quite as small as this, and with the same initials, only reversed." Bea just stared at me then, that faraway look came back into her eyes, staring through me into some past remembrance.

The appetizers came and we barely picked at them but just continued to sip the wine.

After a very long pause, she looked at me, "Do you know what this means?" I nodded. She nodded back and went on, "I don't think they ever wanted anyone to know. I didn't know for years, and even then I wasn't sure. It wasn't out in the open, and no one ever talked about it. I grew up there and didn't know there was anything odd about our family. I usually went to bed before everyone and got up after them. They were early risers. Pete went to work in the morning. Aunt Doris made his lunch. Then Aunt Doris would make breakfast for everyone and Rebecca would help some too. I'd be scuttled off to the bus and after I came home, Pete would come home, kiss Rebecca on the cheek, clean up and we'd all have dinner. Pete would sit in the living room after dinner and read the paper and Doris and your Grandma would clean up and sit in the parlor sewing or knitting or reading. Sometimes Pete would go for a long walk. I'd sit on the floor in the parlor doing puzzles or drawing, then I'd go to bed, sometimes I would still be awake when Pete went to bed downstairs. A little later Rebecca and Doris would go to bed upstairs. I had Doris's room then and Rebecca and Doris would sleep in Rebecca's room, though I'd rarely see them there together. I didn't think it was odd, because it had always been like that. There was no fighting, no strangeness, nor obvious jealousy. We'd go to the fairs, just like other families, go on picnics, go to the beach, we'd just all do it together, and William and Mike often came along. I never knew anything different. I really didn't see anything strange about it until I reached the upper grades, and I visited other kid's homes.

"People didn't talk about what bedrooms they were sleeping in or who they were sleeping with. You did not talk about these things, not in those days. I never said anything to any of them except once, when they said I couldn't have my friend stay overnight. I turned on them angrily and blurted out something about the queer household I lived in. All three of them just stood there looking at me as I stormed out." Bea stopped and we both sipped our wine again. "I didn't even know what that meant when I said it."

This was like a catharsis for her; she was fitting the pieces together that she couldn't even accept before. "It was around that time that I pulled away from them, I guess it was the normal teenage thing, but I began to despise them. I didn't tell them how I felt, I was just silent, I hid in my room and read or went out for walks or visited friends. I only spent time with them when I had to. When we had dinner, I would sit and eat silently, not looking at anyone. Pete would try to talk, try to make things livelier, but then it would fall back into silence again. I know this hurt Rebecca and Doris, Pete too. Sometimes I would hear them talking about it, the women in low, trembling voices; but they never questioned me, never confronted me.

"Eventually, and I mean several years later, Pete got really sick and I finally snapped out of it. I had somehow reconciled with our uniqueness, our oddness. I'd started to see enough of other families to realize that ours was not the worst one around. It was as though a great pall was lifted from the family.

"Overall, they were good parents and were kind to me; they gave me good moral examples. I wasn't isolated, they let me stay at other kid's homes now and then, and they really gave me everything I needed. That's about all I can tell you."

I could only stare at Bea. I'd never heard her open up so before, never heard her talk about her youth. How did she reconcile the fact that her mother loved and slept with her housekeeper for her whole life? Then my next thought was of us, Bea and I and how far we had come and how much I felt like a peer, like an equal in this relationship which before seemed skewed so that I had often felt like a child.

"I know it seems hard to believe that anyone could grow up in that environment and not know, not suspect, not think something was wrong, but I didn't. Well not exactly; I felt we were different, but I didn't feel it was wrong. It seemed as right as any of the other crazy things in the world." Bea shrugged and held her palms up. Then she sipped her wine and stared at the glass pensively.

"I've got Aunt Doris's journal." I said, sipping my wine. "I'm not too far into it, but they met when they were first both working at the mill. I don't know yet how Pete came into it, but they seem to have met before Pete."

"Yes, Rebecca said they were mill girls together." Bea slowly nodded, "Pete worked at the mills too."

I wanted to say, "Can you believe this, it's incredible, isn't it. How can you sit there so nonchalant with this drama that was your life?" But all that came out was, "Well I haven't gotten that far yet." Our entrée came and we ordered more wine, having barely touched our appetizers. The food was good and we continued to talk as we ate.

"I'll make a copy of the journal for you. I have Rebecca's also, but hers seems to have just been of her childhood."

"No, not yet, Honey. You read it and tell me what you want to. I'm not sure how much more I want to know right now. I've got my own memories and feelings about our lives. I'm not sure how prepared I am to hear theirs."

"No problem. So what's on the agenda for tomorrow?" I asked and the mood lightened.

"You tell me. Are you really thinking about buying the old place? What's going on? Would you ever consider moving back here?"

"I don't know, I'm just working it over in my mind right now. I could wake up tomorrow and my thoughts could be 180 degrees away from this."

That evening as I lay in bed, I thought about all that Bea had told me, and about how she seemed so accepting of it and how it was starting to trouble me. How had it affected our lives? Why didn't my mother remarry? Why couldn't I maintain a relationship with anyone? I picked up the journal hoping to get a better understanding.

Chapter 14 - Doris

Tues. Oct 4, 1898

Dear book, I'm writing to Mama and Abigail and Papa tonight, so I won't have very much time. We are all sitting in the informal parlor, some of us sewing, some of us reading, some writing letters and some playing games. It's a quiet evening and as the air is turning brisk I have my shawl on. We're planning an outing for Sunday after church. We'll have our pay and are going to take the trolley down to Norwich and see a play. It is all so exciting and sophisticated, but I wish I had a nicer dress.

Wed. Oct 5, 1898

Rebecca wanted me to try on several of her dresses. After I expressed my distress over my old-fashioned dresses, she wanted to see if any of hers fit me. I knew it was hopeless, as she is about 3 or 4 inches shorter than me and of a smaller build altogether. But I tried to fit into them – to no avail, no matter which style I tried or how hard I tried, I just wouldn't fit into them. It was comical enough that both of us broke into giggles with my arms hanging far below the ends of her sleeves, hem too short and bodice too tight. I was the milkmaid in the princess's wardrobe. Rebecca has such fine and delicate features and arms and legs and hands. She keeps her long auburn hair pinned up because of the machinery, but when she lets it down at night it cascades down her back in shining waves.

I brushed it for her this evening, trying different styles while she held the new ivory mirror from my set and admired my skills with the brush and pins.

Fri. Oct 7, 1898

Our week is almost over, only the half day tomorrow. Oh how excited I am to go to see a real play. One of the other girls of a similar size has given me one of her old dresses that we hope to perk up with some extra trim and ribbons.

Sun. Oct 9, 1898

We're on our way! Yesterday, after we received our pay, I went downtown and purchased a fountain pen, and with this I shall now write. I will no longer be tied to the tables and desks where I can be assured I won't spill my ink bottle. The trolley is comfortable and only jostles us a little, so writing is not too hard. But I don't want to spend all my time writing because viewing the countryside as we go along is a most pleasurable way to pass the time.

Ah! We are now on our return journey and the play was a truly impressive spectacle. It was Romeo and Juliet by William Shakespeare. I have never before seen such beauty. The stage looked exactly as a Roman street and garden. Juliet was so young and beautiful. I imagine that almost any young man would fall in love with her. Rebecca and I both cried at the end and sat there long after the curtain closed. She is sleeping now against my shoulder, the trolley has had such a relaxing effect. We had a modest dinner at a hotel and I felt so very refined and adventurous. I have experienced more in the month I have been here than I or my family has in all my years. I have been at the mill a month tomorrow!

Mon. Oct 10, 1898

I have gotten a promotion and am moving to another floor. I will miss Susan who has taught me so well and little Lizzie, my doffer, who reminds me so much of my sister, Abigail. I will be moving from the winding room to the power looms. The looms are complex and the machinery dangerous if you are not careful, but the pay is very good, and it is a very special promotion for me. Usually it takes a while to go to the looms, but they lost a girl and are moving me in. If I can train quickly I will be sitting pretty indeed. I have a new teacher and helper whose name is Louise. She will be teaching me all of the steps I must follow to weave with these power looms. Sometimes when one of a team needs to go for a break the other spells her for a turn, and in that way they can help one another. I am nervous and excited to start this new training. We are able to gear the machine down some so that I can learn the mechanics of it, but soon it will be put into normal speed so I must learn as quickly as I can so I can prove myself at a slower speed.

Tues. Oct 11, 1898

I stayed a little late tonight to get some special pointers from Louise. We could talk better in the changing room where we leave our aprons and sleeve protectors. When I got home Mrs. Dority had saved a bowl of fine beef stew and several pieces of bread for me. She takes such good care of "her girls" as she calls us. Rebecca had already eaten and Mrs. Dority said she was entertaining a gentleman in the formal parlor, and she tipped her head toward the parlor, smiled and winked. I was very surprised to hear this and it had the odd effect of causing me to lose my appetite, but I quickly finished my supper and dashed off to the parlor. Rebecca and a young man were sitting there with another couple and talking quietly. When I entered Rebecca smiled and both young men stood. Rebecca beckoned me in and introduced us, telling me that Peter works in the machinist's department and used to fix her winder. I shook Peter's hand and told him I was happy to meet him. Rebecca told Peter that I was her roommate and told him of my promotion. Peter looked at me appreciatively. He asked me to join them, and I did. He wasn't a rude or cocky boy, he was nice, and you could see he'd taken a shine to Rebecca. When had that happened? She hadn't ever spoken to me about Peter. After a while I excused myself, and here I am. I need to work on one of my dresses, but I cannot focus. I should read that book from the circulating library before it is due back, but I cannot focus on that either. Why should this bother me so, she is only my roommate, she has a right to do as she pleases. I feel a little betrayed, I thought I was her confidant. I am surprised she hadn't mentioned Peter before. What do I really know of her? She may be as shallow and unpredictable as the rest of the girls.

Wed. Oct 12, 1898

Last night, after Rebecca came into our room, I was already abed. I was rolled over to the wall away from her. She dressed for bed, climbed in and asked if I was still awake. I would not answer at first, but she persisted. "Are you awake?" she asked me. "Yes," I said, "But I'm trying to sleep." "Are you okay? Is everything ok?" Again she asked me. "Yes, just fine." I replied without turning over, but she knows I am not. "Are you sure?" she asked me. "Yes, I'm just tired and trying to sleep," I replied. "We can talk in the morning."

"Okay." She replied, but she knows it is not. As I write this we are in the library. I arrived first and Rebecca sits across the table from me, writing also. I think it odd that she writes tonight, she rarely does, preferring to read the periodicals they offer and an occasional novel. She glances at me and smiles. We have not yet talked about Peter, and I am still confused over the events of last evening.

Chapter 15 - Sarah

Bea was off early again today, but spent a few minutes with me before heading to her part time job at the accounting firm. Bea had been frugal, and even with sending me to college she was able to save enough to take early retirement. But she liked to work and always said that work along with exercise keeps you young, and she looked much younger than her 66 years and seemed more agile, and more alive than many younger people.

"Have you had a chance to think about the house?" Bea, ever to the point, starts out.

"Well, I'm still trying to decide. Do you need to know right away?"

"No, I guess not right away. A couple of weeks won't matter in this market. I haven't even gotten it listed yet. So are you going over there today?"

"Yeah, I'll probably stop down at Jackson's Hardware on the way and ask them what they think about the place and how much work it would take to get it into shape. I mean it's livable, but there are some fairly large upgrades that might make it safer, like the electrical. Know what I mean? I may start going through Aunt Doris's bedroom, too." I was talking between spoonfuls of cereal.

"Yeah, I know it needs work." Bea nodded as she gathered her papers together. "See ya, Honey." She grabbed her keys. "I may stop by later," she said as she sloshed down the last of her coffee and breezed out the door.

I finished up my breakfast, poured another cup of coffee for the road, dug out a pair of beat up jeans that probably needed to be washed and headed out. On the windshield of my car was a note tucked under the driver's wiper blade. I picked it up and read, "Hey would you like to go out for pizza and a beer tonight? – Alice 439-4534."

I reread the note several times, grabbed my keys and went back into the house and called Alice. Somebody at the garage answered and called out Alice's name. When she said hello, I said "Hi, Alice, I'd love to meet you for pizza. How about Angelo's? 6 o'clock?"

"Sure. I'll see you then."

It was exciting to find a new friend. The people I work with are good friends, but after a week with Bea and not seeing anyone else, it was fun to have someone different to talk to. I decided that work friends are like family; they know all about you and you can't avoid spending time with them, and you just have to accept them for who they are. Sometimes there are crushes or real romances that develop, or dislikes and yet, you have to be there with them, day after day. At times they would change for me too; someone I started out disliking became a good friend. This was something different, not a person I'd see every day. I'd be getting to know someone new and have them get to know me, and it didn't hurt that Alice was so easy-going.

I headed out to the hardware store where I got some good advice, and some names of people who could do the work, and they said were fair, competent and reasonable. I'll call one tomorrow and see if he'll come out for an estimate.

It was raining out and the house didn't seem as welcoming as it had on previous visits. Rain, I thought, sometimes it dampened my spirits, but at other times I found it comforting.

I did some more checking around, took some measurements, wrote them down, did a rough layout of the first and second floors, and started making to-do lists and to-buy lists.

I went into Aunt Doris's room, looking about with a new perspective, thinking of the things I'd read. There was a small picture on the dresser of a middle aged woman in an apron, and a young child. It looked pretty old, and I wondered if it was Aunt Doris and her mom. As I opened and closed drawers, gently rifling through them, I discovered they looked much the way Rebecca's did. Some new things she'd been saving, some old and worn things, some treasures she'd probably never worn. I found cheap costume jewelry and a whimsical pin in the shape of a honeybee. There was an old bottle of Channel No. 5, in which the perfume had caramelized on the bottom. In the next, a cotton sock half full of old silver coins and an envelope under that with several one dollar silver certificates. Tucked in the back of the bottom drawer was a cigar box of photos. That will be a treasure trove that I'll save until I get home this evening. It was another day of treasure hunting, and hidden secrets that I wanted to savor.

I stopped by the general store on the way out and used the pay phone to call home. Bea answered.

"Hey, I'm glad you're home."

"Hi, Honey, what's up?"

"I'm meeting Alice at Angelo's for pizza, so I won't be home until later, and I didn't want you to worry."

"Oh." Bea sounded surprised and disappointed, "I was going to fix us some shrimp. I thought that would be fun … I guess I'll put them back into the freezer."

Ah, Mothers, they sure know how to make you feel guilty. "Sorry, it was sorta last minute. How about tomorrow night? I could pick up some Chianti and we could cook up some spaghetti, throw in the shrimp and a little garlic and make evening of it?"

"Sounds good, Honey, be careful, OK?"

"Yep, see you later."

I picked up a newspaper and headed over to Angelo's, dirty jeans, dirty hair and all, thinking "What are girlfriends for if you can't be comfortable with them?"

I got there early and sat down at a booth and ordered coffee. The paper was the little town daily, but I still liked it, local news mostly, but pretty even-handed in their politics. I flipped through it and found the classifieds, poking through the help wanted ads. And there it was: the perfect job.

"Newspaper needs new markup and layout artist. Experience a plus. Centrally located, good benefits, comfortable atmosphere. Call to make an appointment at The Courier News."

I couldn't believe I was even contemplating it – I was so settled in Boston. I had an apartment, a job, friends, and boyfriend. Well not exactly boyfriend. Joe and I never really clicked; it was just an excuse for each of us to have someone to go out with. Most of my friends were married so it was awkward to go out with them or to their homes alone. I always felt like the third wheel, and then there was the other angle, the pressure of them always looking for someone for me. The whole idea of a new life at once frightened and yet excited me. Was I moving too fast to reflect on how uncomfortable it might be, back in the town where I grew up? How would it be to see my mother all the time? Although, Bea seemed to be behaving better than I ever remember, so maybe that wouldn't really be an issue. But maybe once I was back here she'd do an about-face, not wanting me to reflect badly upon her – it must be easier when your children move away. You could tell people whatever you want about them, you could fabricate. "Oh, yes, Johnny's got a great job, he's the Vice President of his firm," even though in reality Johnny might be vice president in charge of janitorial supplies. Maybe it wasn't just Bea who was behaving better, maybe I'd changed. I certainly know I've become independent, and that makes a difference in a parent child relationship. I wasn't relying solely on my mother to affirm my self-worth.

"Hi!" I started as Alice slid into the booth opposite me. She was looking more spruced up than I had seen her before, nice blouse, nice jeans, boots that looked equestrian-like, with her hair down and not pulled through the back of her cap.

"Hi" I said, feeling a bit awkward because I had not gone to Bea's to clean up and change. "You look nice."

"Thanks. Whatcha reading? Any big, breaking stories?"

I snorted, "Nope, just the Smith's cat up the tree sort of thing, you know the stuff."

"I love it, nothing like the local news." Alice motioned to a waitress, "Excuse me, waitress, could you get me a draft? You want a beer, Sarah, or are you going to nurse that coffee?"

"Sure, I'd like a draft, too."

The beer came and we made more small talk about the town and who we knew, and who moved out and back in, who was cheating on who, and all the harmless gossip we could remember. Even though I had been out of town long enough to feel somewhat out of touch, I could still appreciate the spirit of it. Alice grew up in a nearby town and we shared the same high school and knew some of the same people and places, and although not in the same class vaguely remembered each other from school.

"So, what *were* you reading in the paper? The personals?" Alice asked after the pizza arrived and we were working on our first slices.

"No" I chuckled, "The help wanted."

"Oh, really? Are you looking for a job, are you thinking of moving back this way?" Alice scrutinized me. "You are, aren't you?" I nodded with my mouth full.

"But I could use the personals too," I mumbled with my napkin over my mouth.

Now she laughed, raising her eyebrows. "Really, I would think you had suitors lined up around the block."

"Right," I smiled. "Right, that's what everyone is saying to me lately, but the line doesn't exist. I guess I'm just not ready yet, so I scare everyone away, or maybe my mother's poor luck in the husband department soured me."

"Hmmmm, are you thinking of moving into Rebecca's old house? A lot of changes, isn't it... new house, new job? Are you running from something?"

"That's a good question, and one that I've been asking myself. You're pretty intuitive; maybe you should be a fortune teller, or a shrink," I quipped. I liked the easy banter and found myself opening up to her and telling her about finding Rebecca's and Aunt Doris's journals. She listened intently with appropriate nods, raised eyebrows and questions. But I didn't give her all the details or tell her about the rings.

"I'm think I'm going to try and find the journal Rebecca was last writing in, and tie it all together."

"Well I hope you keep me up to date, it sounds intriguing."

"You bet. Hey, if I decide to go ahead with the house, do you know anyone with carpentry, or electrical skills?"

"Well," Alice pushed her plate with the crust of pizza on it away, and signaled the waitress for another beer. "I've done a little remodeling myself, and while I'm not electrician, I haven't electrocuted myself, or burned anyplace down yet either. I could help some, if you want."

"That would be nice." Trying not to sound too pleased and then wondering why that would matter. Two more beers came and we made more small talk until we agreed to meet later in the week after I'd made my final decision about the house.

When I got to Bea's she was already in bed, so I went up to the guest room and opened Doris's Journal, reading the last entry where I had left off. Then, getting Rebecca's journal out, on the hopes there would be a clue, I fanned through it. I had only read a little of it, and sure enough, about a third of the way in, the writing changed to a more assured style and the color of ink was a darker blue, and I thought, how lucky can you get?

Chapter 16 – Rebecca

Wed. Oct 12, 1898

Aye, me. I am so troubled. When Colleen left to go home with the pleurisy, I was so very saddened. She brought to me the brightness of sunshine and when she left, the light went out and my world became a dark and mournful place. When Doris was moved in with me, I was at first vexed. Where Colleen was small and fine with dark hair, Doris was tall and sturdy and blonde, so very different. But now I have grown so fond of Doris, I am fearful she will find me out to be too attached. I have enlisted the help of my friend, Peter, to keep her from knowing the truth, but it becomes more difficult. We are thrown together in such intimate circumstances and spend much of our free time in each other's company. I do so enjoy spending time with her. I am afraid if she knew how fond of her I am, she would spurn my friendship. I look at her now, so serious, so lovely, her blonde hair still swept back from the day's labor at the mill. Her brow furrowed and cheek pale. Oh, how I would love to stroke that cheek. I smile and she smiles back. It is with joy that I respond when she asks to brush my hair and fuss with it. I imagine the touches on my neck as caresses, the accidental brushing against my cheek as deliberate. I find silly excuses to sit next to her or touch her, looking for ways when we plan to spend the day together to hold her arm or whisper gossip into her hair. I fear she will think these imaginings unhealthy and will look for another roommate, another friend, if she only knew, but many of the girls have an intimate. She puts her new pen away, a signal she is done. Now we will go back to our shared bed where I have spent many sleepless hours listening to her deep, even breathing in the night, wondering if my arm, thrown carelessly against her, will cause her to wake.

Thurs. Oct 13, 1898

We are together again, in our parlor, Doris and I, each of us writing in our diaries. She seems to enjoy this time when we both sit across the table and quietly pass our time. I think she likes that I am writing too. I'm planning to go out with Peter for a walk downtown on Saturday. I'm hoping she will encourage this. Then, when she and I go out after to the revival meeting, she will feel as pleased as a friend would when faced with another's good luck in finding a beau. Peter is a good boy, a man really, who likes me and seeks to please me in my whims. I feel I can tell him almost anything, as I would a bosom chum, how unlike most boys. I long to tell him the true reason for spending time with him, as I can tell no one else. When I look around the room at all the others sewing or reading or writing, I can only compare them to Doris, and it seems so unfair because there is no comparison, for she is the blossoming flower among the weeds. I miss seeing her on the mill floor, now that she has moved to the looms. We often get to the dinner table at different times because of this, so I cannot always be guaranteed a seat near her during meals and find myself cross when this happens. Ah, the pen is capped, the signal to retire, oh sweetness of sleep next to my Doris.

Fri. Oct 14, 1898

I am hoping to discover another trip we might take together. I hope to do things that will bring Doris along willingly and where we can be free to enjoy each other's company. I would not want the other girls to become suspicious of our friendship, as Esther had seemed suspicious of Colleen. I'm hoping that the stroll downtown with Peter tomorrow will also help with that. I will be sure to make it obvious to them when he calls to walk me downtown. The evenings grow dark earlier now. I want to get back before dark with Peter so that Doris and I can get started on our outing to the revival meeting before it gets too late.

Sat. Oct 15, 1898

I have gone out with Peter and returned but Doris is not here. Mrs. Dority said she went out abruptly after I left, not saying where she was going or when she would be back.

It is 7 o'clock now and the supper dishes have been cleaned up and still Doris has not returned. I have searched our room for a note or clue of where she may have gone as she did not give me cause to believe she had other plans.

Now I am concerned, as it has just struck 8 o'clock. We have missed the start of the revival and if she doesn't return here before 10 they will lock the doors and she will be reprimanded.

I must go out and search for her. I must.

Chapter 17 – Sarah

"Hi, I know that it's late, but I can't stand not telling you. I am so excited about the journal." I whispered this into the phone when Alice answered, sounding sleepy.

"What?" she drew the word out in a slurred half whisper.

"I'm sorry, I woke you didn't I? I'm really sorry, I was just so excited because I found the rest of Rebecca's journal, and it is just incredible, you go back to bed now."

"Oh sure, wake me up and then tell me to go back to bed. Now I know what kind of friend you are." I could hear her smiling behind the words.

"I'm going to stay." I said this before I thought about it, before I had even made the decision. "I'm going to buy the house." I hadn't felt so sure about anything in years.

"Wow." Alice's voice was becoming clearer as she shook the sleep off, "That was a quick decision, what made you decide? And what time is it anyway?"

"I don't know what made me decide; maybe it was Rebecca. It's 10, talk to you tomorrow?"

"Yep, for sure, but don't call too early, I need my beauty sleep."

I hung up thinking of Alice, and Rebecca, and Doris and Bea, knowing I would need to get some sleep too, if I was going to get a new job and a new house.

When I got up, Bea had the coffee made and was toasting some bread. The rain of last night was gone, and the day was clear.

Bea had the radio on in the kitchen and was humming along, when she stopped and said, "How was your evening? Angelo's has good pizza. Did you have a good time with Alice?"

"I'm going to buy the house." I couldn't slow for the niceties, I was too excited. Geeze, I felt like a kid leaving home for the first time, but instead I was coming home. Bea turned slowly, wiping her hands on the dish towel thrown over her shoulder, and just surveyed me.

"Are you sure this is the right thing? Isn't it kinda quick?"

"Well right now, I'm not sure when I'm moving back, but I would like to someday, so why not buy it? I mean, the history, the sentimental attachment, and I hope to get a break from the owner." I smiled and batted my eyes at her. She looked a little relieved at that.

"Well, Honey, I'm certain the owner would consider your sentimental attachment when pricing out the old place." She smiled back. "I'll go down and talk to the lawyer this morning and see what she suggests, maybe we can circumvent the realtor thing and save you some cash. Then, I swear I will be over to the house this afternoon to help you with Aunt Doris's room. The auction people are coming tomorrow and the shelter people today, so I want to be done and ready for them.

"I may want you to hold onto a few things, so I won't have an empty house to furnish, we'll talk about it when you get there later, ok?" I was hoping to review some of our planned donations to Goodwill and items for the Auction house.

"Sure, I guess we can figure it out then."

After Bea left, I pulled the folded up scrap of newspaper from my wallet and called the number on the ad.

When I hung up, having made an appointment to have an interview, I started to think about clothes. I wasn't prepared for this and would have to get some clothes to wear. I would need to drive back into Boston, or maybe I could get something suitable in Stafford Springs or Willimantic.

As I was standing in my room, trying to decide what to do about clothes, my gaze landed on the journals. I couldn't wait until I could read the next day's entry, only, which one would I start with?

Chapter 18 – Rebecca

Sun. Oct 16, 1898

I do not know where to begin, so much has happened in this last day. Last night, when Doris did not come back, I put on my coat and hat and went out to look for her. Not knowing exactly where to go, I headed towards the library. I ran up the stairs when I got there, interrupting people deep in concentration, even seeing a newspaper held up in an attempt to hide, but pulling it down, found an older lady reading, but no Doris. I left the library and continuing towards the downtown, I passed couples out strolling and an occasional fellow stepping along lively. I could hear the train go by and looked down the street that crosses the bridge where the river drops with a roar as it enters the mill gates to power the machines. There, down Bridge Street, in near darkness, I saw a form leaning over the bridge as if to peer into the water. The figure was barely lit by the streetlamps, but I thought it was Doris. I walked down slowly, as I did not want to frighten her. As I approached I saw it was her, and she turned her head to look at me. I saw her face, dark and shining moist.

"What have you done to me?" she sobbed in a pained voice.

I feigned innocence, and told her I didn't understand. She just repeated herself as I moved nearer.

"Don't. Do not come any closer. I cannot be tortured so, I can no longer stand it."

I reached out to her, but she pulled away and walked further across the bridge. I walked quickly after her and tried to catch her arm. "Please, you must come back to the house, it's getting late, it's getting cold and you could get sick." She turned angrily.

"What do you care? What do you care? You have Peter."

Doris said this with such vehemence I felt I had done a grave wrong.

"I do care, Doris, I care more than you know," I said with all the feeling I could express. She turned and looked long at me with angry, cold eyes. I took her hand and held it in both of mine and as she looked at me, I raised it to my cheek and pressed it there, then put it to my lips and kissed her hand. She made to pull it away, but I held it fast.

"I don't know what we are doing, I don't understand? I am afraid of my feelings and unsure of all I once held right."

"I know," I said. "I understand your confusion. I too am confused, but I know this, I hold you dearer than any other."

"Then why do you go out with Peter, why do you hurt me so?"

"Come home now, we can talk about this as we return, come on." And I led her back toward the house, holding her hand firmly, giving her my handkerchief to wipe her face. I was trying to think of a story to tell Mrs. Dority when we got back so she would understand why Doris didn't come home to supper. Hopefully Doris would not look too amuss and Mrs. Dority wouldn't think it too odd. I talked to her as we walked, asking her what we could use as an excuse. I could feel her hand tighten and loosen in mine as we walked quickly along. "We could say you were looking for a new dress. Or we could say you were studying at the library and lost track of the time. We could say you were talking to Susan about work." At all of these she shook her head.

"I've never had to resort to lying, I don't agree with it."

"Well, what do you propose to say?"

"It will come to me."

When we arrived at the Boarding House, I slipped upstairs before Doris. She stopped at Mrs. Dority's private parlor and told her she had been feeling ill and felt she needed fresh air and walked much further than she had anticipated. Mrs. Dority, being the kind lady that she was, gave her a portion of bread and cheese and told her to sit and eat while she brewed her up some tea. Doris had the bread, cheese and tea, and told our house matron that she was feeling better after the walk and warm tea.

When she came into our room, I was already abed. She quickly got ready for bed and when she got in, complained of being cold and moved closer to me. On this night, after all our nights, I was able to embrace her and pull her close.

So many nights I had dreamt of this, so many nights I spent yearning to hold her. "I didn't exactly have to lie." Was all she said before she turned to me and held me close.

I write this now from the Parlor. We went to our church service this morning, came home for dinner and then went to a lecture at the library. Mrs. Dority was watching Doris for any signs of returning sickness. If Doris became sick she would need to go to the sickroom and be tended for, so that she wouldn't infect the other operatives. The mills were concerned for their workers health as sometimes sickness spread quickly.

All the while I sat with her in the church I would think of the evening before and replay the events in my mind. That is why I can so clearly write them now. When in the church, I can feel the warmth of her arm next to mine. I can only think of last night and tonight. Soon, soon, I will be able to finish up this entry and meet her in our room. I must be nonchalant, relaxed, not hurried and not excited. How hard that is. I look at her and she pauses in her writing and looks up at me and smiles. I smile and make small talk with some of the other girls in the parlor. I find myself very aware of my actions, not just naturally going about my day. I realize that I am not following behavior accepted by our society, and although it feels natural to me, I know others would not accept this. I have become guarded and cautious. How naturally this deviousness comes to me.

Mon. Oct 17, 1898

We are at the library tonight. A long day of work and supper and now we must spend our time busily before we can make our way back to our room. She cares for me and I am so happy about this. She cares for me as much as I do for her. We have spoken of the events that have led us to this, of Peter, and my previous roommate Colleen. I cared much for Colleen, but was never able to express my feelings as I can now for Doris. I have told Peter that I care deeply for Doris and he understands and he cares for me, and wants to see me happy. We talked of the plans we had to keep her from knowing my feelings, which fortunately misfired into such a happy outcome.

I see her finishing up now, wiping off the nib of her pen, folding up her book, putting on her coat. My excitement grows, so much that I want to run back to our room.

Chapter 19 – Sarah

Oh, My, Gracious! This diary, my Grandmother's journal, is beyond my imagination. My Grandmother's journal! My grandmother is a lesbian? How can that be? And she throws herself into it with a passion. It's exciting, scary, confusing. What does it mean? Is this something that can be inherited? I know so little about it and although I had a crush on a classmate in college, I suppressed it, I was afraid of my feelings, afraid to have others know how I felt. Reading my Grandmother's diary brings the guilty feelings back, and yet, I can understand her, sympathize with her. I want to read on and on, and then I want to go back to Doris's journal and get her story, and what a love story! The rings now make more sense, but I want to know more, I want to know how it developed into our little family here. Whoever would have guessed? Two weeks ago I was so blissfully unaware of my family's past. Two weeks ago I was living a simple life in the city.

Am I crazy, thinking that I should be buying this house and moving from my comfortable apartment and stable job? Am I catching this fever from the journals? Is this really how I feel or am I assuming the life and emotions of my Grandmother? If I have to ask these questions, I probably should take some time to reflect. I do weigh decisions, but often go with gut instincts, and they seem to carry me to the best conclusions. Whichever it is, it feels right.

I took a quick shower and raced down to the store to find an outfit for the interview.

When I got back to Rebecca's, the van from the shelter was already parked in the driveway, waiting.

I apologized for being late, but they said they had arrived only minutes before. I let them in and showed them the piles of boxes, bags and small furniture items by the door and helped them shuttle stuff out to the van.

After they left I went up to Aunt Doris's and sat on the bed looking around. It looked so normal. Normal. What did that mean? I looked in her closet again. Old cotton housedresses, mostly clean, but some with sad little stains. Some hat boxes on the top shelf along with folded blankets. A couple of what Grandma would call car coats, one old and worn, one newer. On the floor, several pair of shoes and another small suitcase. We probably should have gone through this before calling the shelter, but then again, there wasn't much, and I could drop it off myself.

Bea drove up and I could hear the car door slam.

"Hello?" she hollered as she came in.

"I'm up here, Ma, in Aunt Doris's room." I heard the screened door slam, and then some rustling and a clunk as she put down some bags, then footsteps as she came up the stairs.

"Well, I've got a good price for you, and we can probably eliminate the realtor. It's not in the best of shape and will need some work to make it comfortable." She leaned towards me as she laid a proposal sheet on the bed with a suggested price circled. "Now remember, this is a deal just for you. If it was on the market I would push it up another ten to twenty thousand, and some realtors would probably push it up more."

I glanced quickly at the sheet and slapping my hand on the bed, playfully declared "SOLD!"

We spent some time going through Aunt Doris's room, piling old clothes and linens onto the bed to be packed up and taken to the shelter. Once in a while one of us would single out an item and comment on it – do you want this? Do you want that? How would this look? We both laughed as I pulled on a hat that looked comical on me, and drew down the dotted net veil and danced around formally. Then I would think about the history behind it. To what affair had Doris worn it? Had Rebecca been there, holding her hand under the tablecloth? Often as we went through her things I thought of her and what she and Rebecca had written. They seemed so far removed from these belongings, I had difficulty reconciling the people in the journal to these old dresses and hats, to the two little white haired ladies. I didn't tell Bea what I was reading; maybe someday. Although she'd been there, she wasn't privy to the underbelly of the relationship, to the reality that they lived day to day.

I started to go through two little drawers on the top of the bureau. More hairpins, old broken hair combs, gold-toned lipstick cases with their contents worn down to the quick. In a fancy compact worn to the metal in the middle with a little line of red powder rimming the outer edge, was some old rouge. There were a couple of sugar packets hardened into odd shapes and some small change.

Then I went to the small secretary and opened it and looked through the papers, which were mostly grocery lists, recipes and a crocheting book. I searched the drawer; it held a dried up bottle of ink, and, pushed to the back, a beautiful old tortoise-shell fountain pen. This pen, it must be Doris's fountain pen, this must be it, the one she wrote that journal with! I felt like an archeologist who has just found the Holy Grail. I was very excited, "Bea, I found a fountain pen in here with some other stuff, is it OK if I keep it?" She barely lifted her head from the box she was pouring through.

"Sure, go ahead. There's not much here worth keeping but some of it is fun to look through isn't it?"

"You bet," was my satisfied reply, as I tucked the pen into my pocket and went on to the other small drawer. I had another connection to them, something to make it all a little more real. There were some brittle, stained and folded letters tucked curiously away in a satin pouch, which I put into my pocket without unfolding, planning to read them later.

An old shoebox revealed photos; some with small riffled edges, some pasted onto stiff cardboard backing, all black and white, including one photo of Doris and Rebecca standing on the porch, with a little girl standing between them. I squinted at the small figures and could almost make out the very young features of Bea. Another of Doris and Rebecca at the beach sitting on towels, wearing old-style bathing suits and sitting under an umbrella, waving.

"There's a bunch of old photos here." I said as I pulled them out and spread them on the bed. Bea leaned over and started to look through them, slowly inspecting each one. Then both of us sat on the bed together looking through the pictures. Bea handed me one she recognized, laughed and said, "I remember this. We went to the sea shore. It was so much fun. Pete put some bologna on a string and I was catching crabs and putting them in my sand pail, then I'd pick one up, carefully the way Pete showed me and chase Rebecca around with it, and everyone would laugh until they cried."

"Geeze Ma, I didn't know you were such a devil."

"Well, I was a little bit of one, but not a bad kid, really. Quite a good one."

Then I found one with Doris, Rebecca, Peter and another man and a boy and a girl.

"Who's this?" I asked, pointing at the people I didn't recognize.

Bea, squinting at it said, "Oh, that's Uncle William and Michael when he was a kid. You know, Michael, Uncle Mike, Harry's dad from the farm next door? And that's me! Here, here, look at this one with Rebecca in that silly hat and Doris and Pete. We were all at the 4th of July parade and Pete was given some crazy paper hats and we all wore them. I took that one myself I had a little Brownie camera."

We sat on the bed looking at pictures for a while before Bea said, "See how easy it is to get caught up in this stuff and not get anything done?"

"We're getting stuff done, Ma. We're reminiscing, talking, and having fun ourselves."

"Yeah, I suppose." Bea said as she started to pile the pictures up.

"Can I keep these? You'll always know where they are, and can look at them whenever you want. But I want to know more about the people I don't know from the photos."

"Sure Honey, bring them along and we can go through them later."

We worked on the room a little while longer then we pulled it together and went back to Bea's where we had leftovers for dinner.

The next day, I went for my interview.

I had bought a neat, casual suit for it, and was showered and dressed before Bea was up. I left her a note saying I'd be back later and went out for a light breakfast and wrote up my resume on a pad while I waited for it. I thought I might be able to stop and get it typed up before I went to the interview, so I asked the waitress if she knew of any local secretarial service, and she was able to give me several names, one very close.

With a typed resume in a 9x12 envelope, I felt confident as I arrived at the newspaper. The receptionist was friendly and had me wait for a few minutes while she got one of the managers. I felt immediately comfortable with everyone I met there. They were welcoming and friendly, and I kept thinking this would be a good fit for me. When they asked me why I was leaving my previous firm I told them that I wanted to get back to my roots; that for whatever reason, I felt a need to come home. I was told they would make their decision in two days and would call me then. I reminded them to call me at my Mothers as I had not yet closed on the house and was staying with her until I could move into it. They spoke words of encouragement that made me feel the two-day wait was just a formality.

When I got back to Bea's, I wasn't sure what to do. I wanted to call my old firm and give them my two-week notice, but then if this job didn't come through, I didn't want to be unemployed either. In the end I didn't call them. I just changed my clothes and settled in to read more of Doris's journal.

Chapter 20 – Doris

Thur. Oct 13, 1898

Last night, as we walked arm and arm back home, I paused to look back at the library and I'm sure I saw Esther quickly draw herself back from the window. Sometimes she makes me nervous, but now, I'm cheered as Rebecca sits across from me and writes again tonight. I do so enjoy our evenings writing and reading. She is being very kind and gives me attentions tonight.

Louise says that I am progressing well on the power loom, learning to draw out all the fine threads. This takes much patience, good eyesight and nimble fingers. I hope to be fully trained in six weeks or so. Louise, who works on the next machine, is able to watch to ensure I am not making mistakes while she still runs hers. She stresses carefulness and quality of work which will save time and give a better product in the end. She says that the machine is geared down slower so that I only need to learn the process, and as I become more agile the machine can be geared up faster.

Fri. Oct 14, 1898

I am hoping to have another adventure after our next pay day. Rebecca promises this but it is a week off, and I must be frugal and put some of my earnings into savings. I will open up a savings account and only allot a fair share for myself. I would like to get some material and fashion a dress to wear to the nicer concerts and special church affairs. I think we are planning to attend a revival tomorrow night and I'm looking forward to getting out after the long week of work.

Sat. Oct 15, 1898

I sit to write now, in our room, I cannot think. I cannot think. I must explain my disturbance. As I was leaving the mill a little late this afternoon for supper, and I was crossing the road to go into the Boarding house, I saw walking away, up the street Rebecca and Peter, arm in arm, chatting gaily and thoroughly engrossed with each other. I am so hurt. Why do I feel thus? I am upset with myself for feeling this way. I am confused as to why I feel so strongly about this. It is hurting me so, my heart is aching. There must be some shortcoming in my nature that has me feeling so. I cannot think and am so confused, I feel ill. I must go out and get some air. Dear book forgive me for being so dramatic, it is unlike me, I know, but I don't think I've ever felt this way before. I must be unnatural, I don't have the desire to have a beau like the other girls, but I am so very touched by Rebecca, she has taken possession of me. Oh, I must get out of this room, it is stifling me.

Sun. Oct 16, 1898

Oh what a day, dearest book. While I wandered yesterday in the depths of despair, walking the streets and feeling more and more distressed, I wondered if indeed this move to work at the mill was the best choice for me. I paused on the stone bridge to look down into the dark swirling water as it raced to the mill. I was frightened by footsteps coming near me and when I turned to look, it was Rebecca. Rebecca, who held my hand and kissed it and declared that she held me dearer than any other. Rebecca, who touched my eyes with her handkerchief, and pressed it into my hand. She does care. She held me close last night and stroked my hair and said she would not ever be so cruel to me again and not to worry. Now my heart soars, now I would kick up my heels but Mrs. Dority would indeed think me ill, as she did last night. How I want to run up the stairs and meet her in our room, but we both must sit here in the parlor, writing and smiling and looking calm, when my soul burns for her. I know this is considered unnatural, but my heart says it is right. I want to touch my lips to hers. I want to kiss her. I have just turned the book to show her these words. She pauses and blushes, pushes the book back to me and averts her eyes. She makes to finish her writing and saying she is tired, retires to our room. As Rebecca leaves and I start to finish up my writing, I see Esther from the corner of my eye, she is taking this all in, the writing, the blush, the warm glances, she is a sly little vixen, watching, watching; or perhaps this is just my overactive imagination.

Mon. Oct 17, 1898

Our innocence keeps us from a sin that could only have us thrown from the church and barred from Heaven. Rebecca cares for me. That is all I know and all I require. She talks of her other roommate and of Peter, but I know that she cares for me. She talks of the many things she wants to do together, of the trips, and visits to her parents. Perhaps a train ride to the ocean, or to Springfield, maybe even New York City one day. I have no preference as to where we go, I would even go with Peter as long as she is with me and we can share our bed in the evening and break our bread together in the day. I have become obsessed, possessed. Oh, happy possession.

Chapter 21 – Sarah

I have become obsessed too. These journals are sucking me into their lives. How fortunate I feel to have the opportunity to read these, to feel their experiences. That they were willing and able to write and save them for so many years just confounds me.

I heard Bea come home and decided it was time to pull myself from my obsession. Maybe I could ask Alice out for dinner. I decided to give her a call.

"Hi, Alice?"

"Hi, how are you doing?"

"I'm good, but I've become hooked on those journals. I need a break, want to go out tonight for a bite and a beer or something?"

"Oh, I'd love to, but I'm busy. Later in the week maybe?"

"Ok, sure. Is everything OK?"

"Yeah, everything is fine, catch you later, OK? I've gotta run."

"OK, later."

"Hi, Ma," I said as I came down the stairs, "What are you doing, want to go out for a bite?"

"Gee Honey, I'd like to, but I'm expecting a call, what were you thinking of?"

"Well, maybe I could go out and get us some pizza?"

"That sounds great, my wallet is over there, grab a 20."

"No, it's on me." I grabbed my keys and was out the door. I don't know why I didn't call the pizza order in, but as I was passing the little bar by Angelo's, I saw Alice's wrecker. I ran into Angelo's and placed our order, then ran out and into the little bar. As I went in and my eyes adjusted to the dim light, I could see her, Alice, with her arm over the shoulder of that other woman, head tilted towards her, talking low and looking serious. They didn't see me, so I slowly turned around and went back out. Alice and another woman. I felt a little twinge of jealousy that surprised me. My excitement over the house, and the job and the journals seemed to go from a full boil to barely a simmer. What was I doing? I had to ask myself.

I walked slowly back to Angelo's and waited for the pizza.

When I got to the house, Bea was in the kitchen with someone.

"Hi Honey, remember Harry? You know, Mike's son? I ran into him yesterday and invited him over, I hope you don't mind, it was short notice and I forgot to mention it…"

I had wanted to have a quiet evening reflecting on the day, thinking about Alice and her friend. I wasn't prepared to have to socialize, especially with someone I didn't even know. Harry walked over and shook my hand. He was tall and thin and attractive in a bookish way. He was slightly stooped and wore glasses; he could be the caricature of a younger absent-minded professor.

"Hi," I said as cheerfully as I could muster. "I hope you like pizza. I got the grand with pepperoni, onions and mushrooms."

Bea whirled around the kitchen collecting plates and napkins and getting us drinks.

Harry said nervously, "So, Bea tells me you're thinking about the house? It's a great old place. My grandfather owned it and sold it to your grandparents. That almost makes us family." He smiled at me as he pulled the strings of cheese away from the pizza slice. Bea was digging in, acting as though she were intent on her pizza.

"I should have been a farmer, at least that's what my father says; as the first born I would have inherited the farm. But when I had serious influenza as a kid, and spent some time reading "The Yearling"; well, I got hooked on books and animals, so I ended up becoming a vet. Dad didn't mind that so much, but Charlie got the farm, since I couldn't manage both a practice and a farm."

Harry was not as shy as he had seemed, and he was genuine and comfortable, I liked him.

We visited for a while and when he left, I literally collapsed on the couch.

Bea had a nose for moods, like bloodhounds have a nose for scent.

"What's going on? Something up? You seem kinda down."

"No, nothings up, I'm fine, there's just so much going on in the last few weeks, I feel like I've been caught up in a whirlwind."

"Well, you know you can always talk to me if you want to."

"Yeah, thanks, Ma." And I really meant it.

The next morning Bea was up and had a couple of soft boiled eggs made with seeded whole wheat toast; she knew this was my favorite. While we were diving into this with some nice French roast brewing, the phone rang and Bea answered.

"It's for you," Bea said as she handed the receiver over to me.

"Hi, OK, yes, OK, yes, sure, thanks for calling." I said as I hung up.

"Who was it?" Bea, asked, ever the curious.

"Somebody from work, I said, I've got to get back," I lied. I hadn't gotten the job. They had given it to someone who lived in the area. They were very sorry, but would keep me in mind if another position opened up. Right.

I needed to get my bearings. I needed to get back to reality.

"I've got to get back to work, Ma, I'm going to leave in a little while, but I'll be back once you decide when the closing will be."

"Ok, Honey, I'll sure miss having you around. Give me a call when you get in, so I don't worry, OK?" She gave me a hug from behind my chair.

"Yep, I will."

I finished up, washed the few dishes and went up to pack my stuff up and put it in the car. Bea hollered goodbye as she left before me. I gathered all my stuff, and my new outfit. I carefully packed the journals and the pictures, the ring box with Doris's ring in it and the fountain pen.

As I drove away, I detoured past Rebecca's, how sad and lonely it looked. Then I headed out to the highway and the drive back to Boston.

Chapter 22 – Doris

Thurs., Oct. 20, 1898

The girls talked excitedly about the upcoming dance at the Lebanon Grange. Esther wanted to know if we were planning to go. I told her I was and thought that Rebecca was also. She said she was going and hoped to join the Virginia Reel with us and some of the others. With a little smile, she touched my hand and said "Save a Dance for me". I could only stare at her in disbelief. What was she proposing? What was she thinking? It made me shudder to think of what she was imagining or what she might know. I only smiled and nodded my head, so taken aback I was.

Sun., Oct. 23, 1898

Yesterday, we bounced our way up to the Grange in large wagons, laughing and singing and talking excitedly. The Elms had sponsored two wagons and several others were coming from Willimantic and I heard from other towns too. A fiddle band was warming up as we arrived and tables of punch and cookies were laid out for us. Rows of folding chairs were lined up around the perimeter of the hall and as we filed in, groups gathered, girls who knew each other collected and giggled and flirted. Boys from the mill and local farms and factories stood on the other side looking shyly at the girls and trying to seem mature and nonchalant. I saw Peter come in with several mill workers and wave at us and Rebecca waved back. The music started and several girls danced together, but the boys still bunched in knots seeming to have important information to share with each other. Finally the caller announced a reel and had the boys all line up in a row on one side and the girls line up in a row on the other. There were more girls than boys and to even it out, the boys line was completed with girls. I stood next to Rebecca. Peter and Esther stood in the line across from us. The dance started and we were made to bow to the people opposite and bow to those on our sides, we do-si-doed and swung our partners across the aisle, in groups of four we circled round and on and on this went until we were warmed up with our first dance. Dances progressed like this with short breaks between where we could get some punch and I think the boys snuck out to sip some brandy and smoke a cigarette. We all started to get wilder and sillier as the dances became faster paced and the caller, we could tell was enjoying the scene he created, his fiddle strings were getting frayed. I found myself paired up with Esther more and more and Rebecca paired up with Peter. Esther was smiling and throwing herself into the dances and holding my hand between sets. This was not odd, for girls to hold hands or walk arm in arm, but it felt strange to me and I was fearful of her attentions, especially when I only want to have Rebecca at my side. Esther sat by me in the wagon on the way back, while Rebecca and Peter sat together. Esther made to hold my hand, but I used the jostling of the wagon as an excuse to break free, but she still was able to briskly kiss my cheek as we all departed the wagons and crossed the street to the Elms in the semi dark. I was discomforted by the evening.

Mon. Oct 24, 1898

Esther again tries to insinuate herself between Rebecca and me. And makes it a point to sit next to me at all the meals and talk exclusively to me. As much as I try to station myself in a position to avoid this, she finds a way to squeeze in. Rebecca finds it funny, and when we are in our room she pretends to be Esther, fawning over me and grabbing at my hand and squeezing in next to me and then laughing over it all. She takes this much too lightly. My only respite seems to be writing here in the library, at least then, even with Esther here, I'm left to write in my book.

Chapter 23 – Sarah

It felt strangely foreign to be back at my apartment, everything familiar and where I left it. Yet, I didn't have to tell Bea where I was going every time I went out, or check in, or plan my life around another person. I didn't really mind doing that, but I had gotten accustomed to my freedom and enjoyed it.

I went back to work and was welcomed heartily. Everyone expressed their sympathy for the loss of my Grandmother.

This was sanity. This was reality. This was good. What was I thinking? I felt like I had gotten so out of touch with reality.

When I went through my mail, I found a note from Joe. He said that after some reflection, he didn't feel we were suited for each other. He said he liked me, but wanted to move on, and hoped, and expected that I wouldn't mind. He said he tried to call me and that he was sorry about my Grandmother. That was it. It was surprising. And a bit hurtful, but I thought sooner or later one of us would have ended it. He was right, I didn't feel too badly, but piled on top of the other difficult things I'd been experiencing lately it felt like another little weight.

I was busy catching up for the first few days. At work I was trying to get back into the rhythm of the job, laying out ads took little thought after having done it for years, it came as second nature to me, but being away for a few weeks seemed to slow my pace. At home I was returning calls, as well as cleaning around the house, doing laundry and answering sympathy cards. By the end of my first week home, my life felt like it was almost back to normal, and good to be busy so I didn't have to focus on what I wasn't ready to deal with.

I called Betsy and Maureen and talked for a while, hoping for an invitation, and thankfully they asked, they were having a few friends over for dinner, could I come? You bet.

Saturday rolled around and after I finished my errands and did laundry that had backed up; I went over to Betsy and Maureen's, friends from work, lesbians who had been together for a number of years now. I was excited because I thought they would be interested in the journals.

Sophie and Sol came and brought a pot of Borsch and a loaf of sour dough that she was well known for. I brought several wines and we all sat down to a sumptuous dinner.

They asked me about Bea, and how we both were doing, and what else I was up to.

"Well, I might be buying my Grandmother's house."

"What? So nonchalant? Are you moving away? I can't believe it" Betsy erupted. "Tell us. Tell us everything."

"Everything is a much longer story than we have time for, I'll give you the condensed, but still engrossing version. Bea and I started cleaning out Grandma Rebecca's old homestead when I came across a wedding band in a ring box. It was simple and sweet. I tried it on, but then I put it aside to give to Bea. As I kept cleaning, I came across a few nice heirlooms like an ivory comb and brush set, and a few other things. Then I found Rebecca's journal, and a quick peek seemed to show it was a diary of youthful experiences, which was cool." I paused to sip my wine.

"Well, not long after, I came across Doris's journal. You know, Aunt Doris was her house keeper; it was kind of hidden and marked personal. Hmmm… I was thinking this could be interesting. So I tucked it away and kept up my task of cleaning out the house. The house, by the way, is an old farmhouse style, with the big wide porch, in a tiny village on a fairly quiet road, not in the best of shape, but sound enough, and can be lived in while renovations are done."

"Anyway, I read a little of Rebecca's diary, and it was sweet and talked of her rural youth. Now, here's the interesting part. When we went to the funeral home, the funeral director gave me Rebecca's ring."

Betsy and Maureen glanced at each other, raised their eyebrows, then turned back and focused on me. Sophie paused to butter a piece of sourdough and lean in as I continued.

"I put the ring on, puzzled, because I thought I had her ring back in the box at Bea's house. That evening, when I got back to Bea's, I looked on the inside of the ring from the funeral home and it said, 'FROM DB TO RM WITH ALL MY LOVE'. DB, I thought to myself, who the hell… then it dawned on me Doris Biracree. RM was of course my Grandmother, Rebecca Moorhouse."

Betsy and Maureen looked stunned. They sat with their mouths open, looking from me to one another and then back to me. "Oh my goodness" came from both of them at the same time. Sol reached over and put his hand on Sophie's who sat transfixed.

"So the next thing I did was go to the ring box that I found in the drawer and it said, RM TO DB, LOVE OF MY LIFE!"

There were more jaw-dropping looks all around. Sol said, "So a little secret in your family?" Sophie glanced at him and nodded her head in agreement.

"I knew you would appreciate this. Can you believe it? Well, that's just the start. After I saw this it all started to sink in, so I started reading Doris's journal, and you know what? They met at the mill when they worked there as mill girls and lived in the boarding house together, sleeping together. I guess in those days it wasn't uncommon in boarding houses to sleep two in a bed. So far, it seems like my Grandmother Rebecca may have been in a close relationship with Doris, she may even have been bi-sexual. I don't know for sure, I don't have all the details yet, and I may never have them. It sometimes still just floors me. I haven't finished the journals, it's a little slow going in Doris's longhand, so I don't know how it ended up the way it did, with the women in the house with Pete, and then my mother coming along. I hope they have some of it in the journal, because you can't make this kind of stuff up, it's just too unbelievable."

Betsy clapped like a kid, "I'm so excited, I want to see those journals, when are you going to release them to my custody? I promise to take good care of them. What a treasure! How lucky you are!" Maureen seconded the sentiment. "Yes, I can't wait!"

Sol cautioned, "Be careful of them, do you have a way to make copies?"

We talked on and on about women's journals and women's writings, women's histories, women's stories, and what a find the journals were.

Then talk turned to me, and my lagging love life.

Betsy, ever direct, asked, "So, how about you? Still seeing Joe?"

"Well, no, not as of yesterday. Really, we'd hardly been seeing each other before I went away, but now, well, he's moved on. I really don't feel too bad, but it was nice to have someone to go out with once in a while; it was no great romance. Oh well." I drifted off.

Betsy, still on the trail followed up with, "So, there's nobody in the wings

"Betsy." Maureen was using her you're-being-naughty voice, "You pry too much. I'm sure if Sarah wanted to share anything with us, she would." She finished off with a snort and a head shake.

"So, is there anyone?" Betsy wouldn't let go.

Sophie followed up with, "Come on, no one? Not even a friend you're fond of?"

"No. And I'm not sure how interested I'd be, you know. I'm kinda used to being alone, to having my own…"

"Aw, that's hogwash," Betsy interrupted. "That's what all the single people say when they can't find the right one, and they always think there is a right one, a perfect fit. There probably is someone, somewhere, but why be so discriminating? It blows my mind that in some cultures the parents still choose the intended spouses, and you know what? Most of those marriages work. You wouldn't think that would make sense would you, but, people make things work if they want to, or not, if they don't. It's that simple."

"Ok, Betsy, we've gotten your sermon for the evening, thank you, it was very illuminating." Maureen was trying to get Betsy off the band wagon.

"Well, did you ever think about women?" Maureen picked up where Betsy left off. Sol stopped chewing and looked from Maureen to me.

"Actually, when I was in college, there was someone, and I was smitten. I've never told anyone about it. I was infatuated. She was pretty, but it was not just that. She also had a presence about her, a sort of dynamism. Everyone liked her and wanted to be around her; I was just one of many. I'd steal glances at her in class, hoping no one would notice, especially her. When she asked me to go out for a beer one evening I was almost ready to swoon. I actually imagined she might like me in more than a friendly way. I was entertaining *those* kinds of thoughts, ones that I'd never had before. But when we went out, she'd talk about this upperclassman she was interested in and how he wasn't interested in her, she went on and on about him. And my impossible dreams were smashed. Oh I still dreamed about her, but never, ever told her, or anyone else, for that matter. And she would occasionally still ask me out for a beer, and I would go, and just bask in her company, but it was not to be. We graduated and I didn't see her again. End of that story." I stopped to have another sip of wine. "And, well, sometimes I think I'm just not good at being with someone. I'm not driven to get into anything that isn't meaningful, and I haven't found anyone who fit in that meaningful way."

Sophie smiled at Sol and said, "Well, I think there's someone out there for everyone." Everyone besides me, murmured in agreement.

They didn't press me any further on it. We gabbed and gossiped and sipped wine until we were all yawning; fortunately I didn't live too far away.

"Well everyone, it's been lots of fun. Now promise me that when I start working on the house you'll come out some weekend and give me a hand, or at least just come and hang out."

"You bet, count us in!"

That evening I went home and for the first time in days, opened the journals.

Chapter 24 - Doris

Tues. Oct 25, 1898

Please keep this secret, and destroy it if you have read it.

Last night we retired as early as was suitable, and we were readying for bed when Rebecca said, "Remember what you wrote the other night? About kissing me?" I said I did, and she said that I should do it if I wanted. She walked to the window and closed the curtain and walking back leaned against the bed. I walked over to her, the fear and anticipation and excitement almost overcame me. I took both of her hands and leaned to kiss her lightly on the lips. That kiss I will never forget and I play it in my mind over and over again. I have been kissed before, a boy kissed me once, and I could not understand the excitement over it. But finally, I understand, it was as if a shock ran between us at that tiny spot where our lips met. I felt as if the focus of all my existence was that pinprick of touch where our lips met; it took my breath away. I sat on the bed, almost faint and feeling I was no longer in my body and Rebecca sat with me, fingers entwined with mine.

It was as if it burnt me from my lips to my heart which felt as if it would expand to bursting and my whole body came alive. I had never felt such intense joy. I could have screamed, or cried, or run out shouting. I didn't know if she felt all that I did. I didn't know if she would still want me. Want to kiss again. But it was all I could think of, kissing and kissing and kissing, I could think of nothing else.

The autumn air was chilly as we dressed quickly in our night clothes and embraced in the bed, our thin cotton gowns barely separating our warming bodies. We kissed and embraced until finally, her head in the crook of my shoulder, Rebecca fell asleep.

That was last night, and it was all I could think of all the long day today. That kiss, that passion. We are at the library, but I yearn to be at the room with her and think of how we can contrive to be alone. Soon, soon, the clock just now struck 8:00.

Wed. Oct 26, 1898

What joy I feel when I see her face, when I walk to breakfast and she is there sitting amongst the other girls and she looks to see me as I come through the door, her eyes flashing with recognition. Every time I see her it is a thrill. Sometimes when we are walking back and forth from the mill to the boarding house for meals and back again to work, I see a girl from behind, who looks like Rebecca and it makes me happy. Then she turns and it is someone else, and the pleasure I took from seeing her quickly ebbs away.

Thurs. Oct. 27, 1898

Rebecca is with Peter this evening while I write in the parlor with the other girls. We have agreed that we need to be thoughtful of our actions lest someone become suspicious. I do not like feeling dishonest, but doubt that I have a choice in this. Peter sits with us and we scheme about it. We plan to walk together downtown tomorrow, the three of us, but it is necessary for Rebecca and Peter to sit together in the formal parlor tonight. I am no longer jealous of Peter, and I am no longer fearful of losing Rebecca. I am just joyous at what I have, and that is my dear Rebecca. At every meal I see her smiling and I join her in our bed at night. I can want for little more. But tonight Esther sat with me and talked in a low voice about Rebecca and Peter and how she thought Rebecca a devious girl whose emotions would blow in the wind like a leaf, first this way, then that, and she was inconsistent in her devotion to people. As she talked she was watching me and my reactions, I tried to steady myself and not show emotions, but found it hard not to defend Rebecca, and said once that I thought her a good person. But Esther went on about how Rebecca once turned away Colleen when she found another friend and Colleen became so ill she finally left the mill. I said that I heard another story, but I must say the talk left me uncomfortable. Does Rebecca care for me, or have there been others, are there others? Esther is indeed a dangerous girl.

Fri. Oct. 28, 1898

I told Rebecca what Esther said. I was confused and nervous, fearful of Esther and her conniving and the tiny doubt planted by Esther's insinuations. Rebecca was at first hurt that I would doubt the depth of her feelings for me, but then she became angry with Esther, very angry. She threatened to go after Esther and give her a piece of her mind, but we talked for a while and I was able to calm her down and have her realize what a dangerous position that would put us in. We decided to just avoid Esther as much as possible and pretend that nothing was said. I am going to try not to be left alone with Esther so that she cannot take advantage of the situation.

Sat. Oct. 29, 1898

Peter and Rebecca and I went for a stroll yesterday after supper. The air was brisk and clear and leaves from the trees were down and crunched underfoot. We stopped at the five-and-ten-cent store for a malt, where we schemed some more. Peter thinks we can save up enough money to move into our own apartment, and then with all our pay combined we can save enough to buy a house. It all sounds so grandiose. I cannot imagine it and I am not too keen on having Peter with us. What role could he play? What role does he want to play? Rebecca says to not worry so much, but my future and our happiness is at stake. Tomorrow Rebecca and I are going to the Presbyterian Church together, then after that, we three are going to the Regimental Band Concert at the Armory, which should be a rousing time.

Mon. Oct 31, 1898

The concert was all I had hoped it would be, and we all three marched and sang our way back to the house. We stopped by a flat which had been posted for rent, but the landlady looked at the three of us and said it had already been rented. So fearfully did she look at us that when we left, we ran down the street laughing and making faces at each other as though we were ogres. Peter is a good man, and I am liking him more than I imagined I would.

Chapter 25 – Sarah

The daily routine of my job was comforting, but for the first time in years, I missed Bea. I would give her a call now and then to see how things were progressing, and always with the same response that she and the lawyer had some things in the works and the closing would be postponed for a couple months. So I was happy, when almost a month after I got back to work, there was a note in the mail from Bea asking me to please call her.

I kicked off my shoes, changed into my sweats, and settled down to have a nice chat with my mother. She was home, and pleased to get my call.

"Hi, Honey, how have you been? I've been missing you." We talked about the house and small town news, then, "Hey, somebody called you and I took a message, a newspaper or something. They want you to call them back. I've got the message written down, let me get it." When she came back, she asked, "What's this all about?"

"Really, they called? Hard to say, maybe a job. I'll tell you all about it later, ok?"

The next day, during business hours, I called The Courier News and to my surprise, they wanted me to come back for another interview, asking if I was still interested, and explaining that the man they had just hired wasn't a good fit and had left.

"Yes, I'm interested." We made an appointment for the following week.

As I hung up I wondered if I was acting too impulsively again, but, then decided that I didn't have to take the job. I still had a little while to think it over. After all, I hadn't even had a second interview, nor been offered the job yet.

I asked my manager for the next week off. I had already told her I was buying my Grandmother's home so the prospect of me leaving had probably crossed her mind. When I told her I was considering moving back there, she said she appreciated me being candid about it.

I wandered about the apartment trying to think of what I would bring with me to make it comfortable. I called Bea.

"Hey Ma, how are you doing?"

"OK, how about you, everything OK?"

"Yep. Guess what? I'm coming to visit again. Next week."

"What? Really? What's up?"

"Well, I thought I might do some work on the house. And I was thinking about staying there while I did it. Would that be OK? Do you see a problem with it?" I didn't pause to let her answer, "So, do me a favor, don't get rid of Doris's bedroom set, OK? I think I'll just use that room. What do you think?"

"Wow, you're really serious? You're not worried about the closing or anything? What do you think you'll be doing?"

"Oh, I thought I'd start with a serious cleaning. So much of it just needs cleaning and maybe a little painting. I'll start with the bathroom and upgrade a few easy things like curtains. Maybe even think about new fixtures. You know, stuff like that."

"Well, I think that's fine. I'll come over and give you a hand if you want. Now I almost wish I hadn't gotten rid of Rebecca's furniture. I'll put a hold on the rest if you want; there are those overstuffed chairs in the front parlor and side table, a few lamps, the kitchen table and chairs. I can have them leave all that stuff. I think that should make it livable for now."

"Great, Ma. Thanks for all your help. I'll be coming down probably Saturday evening. Want to have dinner?"

We finalized our plans for dinner and for the week, leaving gaps for each of us to get our own stuff done. We were both excited.

The rest of the week went quickly and I packed up a few nice clothes, some work clothes, bed and bath linens, the journals and the set of tools I had collected for repairs around the apartment. I wasn't a craftsman or a carpenter, but I knew which end of the hammer to use and how a power drill and skill saw worked so I felt I could manage minor repairs on my own.

On Friday I drove out from Boston and dropped all my stuff off at the house, Rebecca's house. Then I went to pick up Bea.

We went to the Steak House a few minutes away. Since we never really celebrated my plans to buy the house, this seemed like the right time;

it seemed more solid now. Probably even Bea didn't think I was serious. She may not have even started the closing process, giving me time to rethink and back out if I changed my mind.

"How long are you going to leave the phone and electric on?" I said over the cheesy Nachos.

"I was thinking about leaving them on," she paused for a sip of her oversized margarita, the glass rim encrusted with salt, "until we turned it over to you."

"Really, that's nice, if you give me the bill for this month, I'll pay it and have it transferred."

Bea nodded and crunched on a salty tortilla chip.

"That girl called, you know." She paused for another sip, "You know, Alice?"

The chip aimed for my mouth stopped in mid-air. "Oh yeah, when?"

"About a day or two after you left to go back to work."

"Huh? When were you going to tell me?" I said, trying not to sound too annoyed.

"I just forgot... and oh, Harry called too." Bea's shoulders and eyebrows went up, using her innocent voice that was employed whenever she was feeling guilty.

"He's a sweetie, isn't he?" I said as I thought about how his serious demeanor made him look older.

Talk turned to the house and what my goals were for the week.

After dinner I returned to the house settled in and started again on Doris's journal.

Chapter 26 – Doris

Tues. Nov 1, 1898

We are at the library again tonight. Rebecca reads periodicals and moves about, not able to keep to one activity. Now she's searching through the books, now watching the tutor giving Arithmetic lessons, now she's flipping through the photography book of World travel. I know what she's thinking, I think the same, but I continue to write because I know we cannot go back to the house yet. Last night we were lost in passion, so wild, so deep, yet silent. As I drifted off to sleep, with Becky's head on my shoulder, I thought I heard Becky whisper something, but it was not clear. Ah, the clock strikes 9, the library closes, we are the first to leave.

Wed. Nov 2, 1898

Last night as we left the library, arm in arm, I looked back and again saw Esther looking out the window, shading the glass with her arm; she did not pull away this time, but stayed to watch us as we made our way back to The Elms.

They are in the formal parlor tonight, Peter and Becky. I am left in the dining room to be a good single girl, while my friend and roommate courts a boy. This is the illusion we would want Mrs. Dority and the other girls to believe. The other girls around me sew and make pleasant banter and write letters home. One of them asks me about Rebecca and Peter, and I tell her, as everyone listens, that they are sweet on each other, and that I think they are a handsome couple. But to myself I think that as a couple they are not as handsome as we are. Why is this so wrong? Why, when we are both feeling this is so right and natural does the rest of the world think it unnatural? It is not fair or right, I determine. Love is right and that is all. Out of the corner of my eye, I catch Esther watching me with an odd look.

Thurs. Nov 3, 1898

I'm at the library again tonight, and again, Becky moves about restlessly. She came to me last night in a passion. This seems to happen after she spends time with Peter. I have asked her why, but she is unable to explain it. She kisses me and pushes me back onto the bed and climbs atop me, presses herself against me and kisses me quite roughly. I do not resent Peter for leaving her so. I thank him. If only he knew. She is to see him again tomorrow night, I can hardly wait, I will retire a little early, I think. Tonight I hope we can rest.

Fri. Nov 4, 1898

Again Rebecca and Peter are in the parlor. I am to write a little and mend a tear in my stocking and do another mending job, chatting with the other girls and then retire. It is eight o'clock and I will stay up until nine. We are planning to go to a poetry reading tomorrow night, Peter and Becky and I, over at the concert hall. It promises to be a lovely evening; we are hoping to go for a malt before the reading. I have my mending to do now.

Sat. Nov 5, 1898

It is over. It is all over. What am I to do?

I sit now in our room, crushed, anxious and of broken heart. Last night, all happened as planned. I finished my mending and went to our room, dressed for bed and waited for Rebecca. I lay in bed waiting, and Rebecca came in directly and to the bed and kissed me, then went to change into her night clothes. She again threw herself into the bed and atop me and kissed me with wild kisses, my face, my neck, my breasts; we were thus engaged when, with a loud bang, the door flew open, and Mrs. Dority stood there with an electric torch, Esther behind her shoulder, craning to see. "Get out! GET OUT!" she screamed at us. We were so taken aback; we didn't know what to do. Rebecca quickly got up and rummaged for her robe. Mrs. Dority spat profanities at us, calling us unnatural. She said she had her suspicions, but when Esther went to her and complained that Rebecca tried to kiss her, her suspicions were confirmed. She said we were disgusting, immoral girls. Rebecca stood there, pleading with Mrs. Dority. We cannot be turned out, she said, we have nowhere to go. "I do not care," said Mrs. Dority. Rebecca begged, but this is not Doris's fault, it is all my fault, all my doing. I will go, send me away, let Doris stay, she is innocent. Mrs. Dority looked from one to the other. Pointing at Rebecca, you sleep in the sick room tonight and find other lodging by Sunday or I will turn you out to sleep rough in the street. You, she said pointing at me, you can stay here until I can figure out what to do with you. Rebecca gathered her belongings and was put in the sick room. I was left behind, shivering, anxious, heartsick and alone, in this once blessed, now wretched room.

Chapter 27 – Sarah

It was a lot like camping out, that first night at the house. The house. I liked how it sounded. It wasn't Rebecca's house anymore; it was The House, My House. I felt comfortable and safe and would have slept fine but for the last day's entry of the journal which was playing through my mind. How frightening. How humiliating. How sad. A budding love affair treated like a crime. I know this is my grandmother, but I'm beginning to feel as though this is someone I don't know, like this is someone else's adventure. I am incredulous at the experiences my Grandmother went through. How can we know what others endure if they emerge somewhat unscathed, having triumphed over their adversity? I had to talk to Bea. I was hoping she might have more to say about her youth and family life. I wondered what her plans were for the headstone. I wanted some part in that. I wanted this enduring relationship honored, and once she read the journals, I thought she would too.

I had the old coffee maker here and had brought some basics from my apartment, so I could have my morning brew and some cereal to get me started. Maybe I'd go out for a grinder at lunch. I sat at the old Formica dinette set, with the chrome-legged chairs, and started a list of what I would need at the hardware store: paint, caulk, scraper and putty knife. A knock at the front door interrupted me. I pushed away from the table, and went to the door to find Bea, who pushed by me with a large bag of bagels in one hand and doughnut holes in the other.

"What did you think? I would let my only daughter start on the first day of her first house project by herself?" She breezed in cheerfully.

"You might have called," I said. "I could have had my shotgun out, ready to shoot the intruder."

"Yeah, right, where is that mythical shotgun, anyway?" Bea, ever the smart aleck quipped, her head going side to side as if to look for it. "What would it be this or this?" she grabbed the broom in one hand and the mop in the other. "The broomstick, I'd definitely go with the broomstick."

"Hey," I said digging into the bag looking for a raisin bagel, "You know those journals?" I found a raisin bagel, then some cream cheese which I slathered onto the bagel. "They are just incredible. Really, they are like historical snapshots of people's lives back then. You know, they had quite unusual and exciting lives."

"Really, do you think I should read them? They wouldn't be too dull for me? I like the faster-paced stuff, you know."

"I think you'd find them, well, enlightening. But let me finish them before I share them with you. I think I need to photocopy them or transcribe them. It would be a tragedy to lose them, or to have them get wet or somehow destroyed."

"I guess." Bea's tone was somewhat dismissive as though that topic was exhausted and she was ready to move on to the next. "So, what's first?"

"I've got a list started here, and I need to go out and pick up a few things. Where do you think is best? Is Brooker's Hardware the best or is it too expensive? It's just so close and I don't want to be traipsing all over just to pick up a few basics."

"Yeah, Brooker's is OK for a few things, but go to that big one in town if you're going to get a bunch of stuff."

"OK, while I'm gone, you can start with the upstairs bath, it really needs some serious deep cleaning. There are still some cleaning supplies that you left, and I brought a box too, some rubber gloves, ammonia, cleanser, sponges, you know, all the necessities. It's in the box in the kitchen.

"I'm going to keep the claw-foot tub because it really is quite a beauty, but I may add in a shower stall, too, someday. Then I can get rid of that metal rod above the tub. I love that it's such a big bathroom; I can do so much with it. I need to pull out that carpet in both of the parlors, though. It really reeks when it's humid. I expect there's some hardwood underneath that I can get refinished. What do you think?"

"I like it. Sounds like you've got some pretty good plans so far. What else are you thinking?"

"Well, I like Pete's room downstairs and I'll probably keep that the same. It's good to have one bedroom on the first floor. That other room behind Pete's I may make into a study. I like the double parlor so I'll probably leave that. The kitchen is good, too, and big enough. I'll bring down my wooden kitchen table and get rid of the Formica."

"Oh, yeah?" Bea interrupted me, "Are you moving down here, moving back from Boston? I thought you were just going to fix this up and rent it out. What about your job?"

"Whoa, whoa, whoa, wait a minute. I may move back." I hated to tell Bea too much sometimes, because if she didn't like it she could give me a pretty hard time, and I didn't need that right now. But I realized I'd have to tell her something. "I'm interviewing for a job this week with The Courier News, so we'll see, a lot depends upon that."

"Really? Hmmm. Is the pay much different?"

"I'm not sure yet, it's probably not the best salary, but you know it's cheaper to live down here than near Boston, so if it's even close, it will be like getting a raise." I was trying to put a positive spin on this, which wasn't hard, because I did feel good about it. I would be leaving my friends, but they could visit. I wasn't into the rowdy nightlife, so I wouldn't miss that. I'd be able to garden again, which I loved, and would be able to landscape to my heart's content with this much land. I'd be closer to my roots, too, which had become more important as I got older.

Bea spent the morning cleaning the tub and around the sink while I started scraping paint off the trim. I was happy for the help and spoke above the scraping and scouring. "Don't worry about making a mess. I'll clean up once you're done."

I paused in my scraping to ask, "So when did you leave home? I don't think you ever told me."

Bea paused, wiped her forehead with the back of her hand and sat back on her haunches. "I went to work at the mill when I was 16 and worked there for about 6 years. Then, with the money I saved and what they could give me, I went to teachers college down in Willimantic. I got a two-year degree. I was living at home the whole time, and I had to take the train in to school every day. When I got out of college, I didn't get a job right away and was still living at home with Rebecca and Pete and Doris. It was hard, but it got harder as the economic depression deepened. We weren't starving or losing our house, but the women started to get paranoid about every little sliver of soap; they made me crazy. Of course, I didn't have to pay the mortgage, so still, even in my late 20's I didn't understand how much they had to sacrifice to pay the bills and help me. Finally I couldn't stand it anymore and when I met your father, well, it was my way out of the house and I married him. I didn't love him, but people got married in those days, they didn't live together, and they rarely got pregnant outside of marriage. Then, you came along, and you were what held me together. You might think a struggling couple wouldn't want another mouth to feed, but you just, well, sort of completed me." Bea leaned back into the tub and scoured some more and then turning on the squeaky tap swished some of the dirty water down the drain. "I was able to get a job right after you were born. I was really lucky and I worked nights while you stayed with your father. Sometimes you stayed with Becky and Pete and they loved for you to visit. But once you went to school, I was able to go to days and I got a job in the accounting department, and well, got a life without him." Bea was matter of fact, not one to feel sorry for herself or lament her choices; it was one of the things I admired about her.

We worked a little longer then stopped for lunch.

"I'm hoping to finish scraping the trim in the bathroom and sand it down enough so I can put on a coat of paint today. Put shower curtain on that list in front of you, the one upstairs is really pretty bad. I'm going to toss it. Can you stay and do a little painting?"

"Sorry, Honey, I'm busy this afternoon, but I may be back tomorrow morning if you promise me the broomstick won't be loaded." She smiled and drained her soda.

"OK, OK, you laugh, but you gave me a fright. I may just get a gun. Then what would you do? I bet you wouldn't come waltzing in anymore without any notice."

"I just wanted to surprise you, Sweetie. Promise I won't pop in again without advance notice, OK?"

Bea left and I continued my scraping and sanding. I hated scraping and sanding and painting, but done right, it really made things look good. I was in mid-scrape, when I thought I heard a knock at the front door. I pulled down the bandana I had over my nose and mouth and listened. Nothing, back to scraping, but there, again, I'm sure it was a knock. I wiped my hands on my stained jeans, pulled my dust mask down around my neck and went down stairs, stomping the dust off as I went.

I opened the door, expecting Bea and wondering why she didn't just march right in.

"Hi, can I come in?" Alice, looking a little chagrined, stood still for a second, with an armload of grocery bags, before I stepped aside and let her into the hall.

Chapter 28 – Doris

Sun. Nov 6, 1898

Alas, I am in purgatory, I am in hell. I sit in my room, writing on my band box. Waiting to know what my fate will be.

I can barely sleep or eat. I have no desire for either, but am tortured by my fate. I lay awake in bed all night reviewing the last few days, how horrible it was, how horrible it is. I held Rebecca's pillow and smelled her scent on it, and cried, then finally after untold wakeful hours fell into a fitful sleep. Yesterday morning Mrs. Dority came to my room and told me I can go back to work, that I must eat in the parlor, and not to socialize or in particular to speak to Rebecca if I saw her. She said that if I did not do these things, I could pick up my belongings and leave. She was planning to talk to the mill bosses on Monday and would come back to me with their decision on what was to be my fate.

This morning she told me to go to church and pray for forgiveness and to eat quietly at the small table in the dining room, not socializing with anyone. I have not seen Rebecca since Friday last. I am so touched and proud that she defended me, and lied to protect me. It proves to me more and more of her commitment, and makes me steel my resolve to hold fast against my fears in the face of this assault upon our love. My uncertain future is in the balance.

The other girls this morning sat at the long tables with their breakfast and talked brightly and stole glances at me and then whispered between themselves and tittered. I am now an outcast; I am now to be shunned. Esther led the flock as she turned up her nose and looked away from me. If I am able to keep my room here and my job, it will be of little solace, as I will have no companionship to bring me comfort.

Mon. Nov 7, 1898

The mill seemed different this morning as I walked to work with the other girls. The large brick buildings with the windows upon windows seemed colder, more austere. The people seemed to be less friendly as I donned my apron and arm covers in the changing room. I felt that everyone knew my secret and was watching me. The large, wide, worn wooden staircase up to the third floor where I worked echoed more than usual. The machines seemed louder, the dust thicker, and the smells of oil from the machines hung over all. Leather belts, burned from driving the machines, smelled more acrid, and even the overseers seemed harsher. The stool where I sat to work in front of the machine seemed harder. The world seemed to be against me and I was sore of spirit. When the dinner bell rang and we all trouped back to the boarding house for our meal, someone came up behind me and pressed a note into my hand. I turned to see who it was, but did not see anyone I knew, and no one looked to recognize me. I put the paper furtively in my pocket. Back at the boarding house, I forced myself to eat because if I became sick I would have been sent home.

When I took a moment to go to visit the toilet, no one looked, and I was able to read the note. "We are scheming to affect your escape, hold tight, all will be made right." I didn't recognize the handwriting, but was in no doubt that it was from Rebecca and Peter. Although I didn't know what had happened to Rebecca and I was worried for her outcome, the note put me much at ease.

Mrs. Dority took me aside after supper this evening and said the mill was willing to keep me on, but I was not to socialize with anyone. I was to go to my room after I return from work or to the library for several hours in the evening, but was expected to return to my room. I would be on probation until they thought I was summarily disciplined and was contrite for my unspeakable behavior.

I consented to this, even though in my heart I did not agree, nor believe I had done anything wrong, but for the time being, it was all I could do.

Tues. Nov 8, 1898

I was brought to the office of an agent of the mill today.

He had me sit in one of the chairs, out of the way of the window that he watched the workers from. I was lectured to, and made to read the letter of agreement that I signed upon starting work at the mill. Girls at this mill, he said, were required to be hard working, clean, church going and morally upright. If we did not keep to that standard, he reminded me, the fathers of the good girls from the farm and country homes would not allow their daughters to be sent to the mills. He told me that any indecency or immorality would not be tolerated, that this was my warning, and did I understand?

I answered meekly that I understood, and that I was sorry for my transgressions. He looked stern, but seemed satisfied that I had learned my lesson. He said I should work hard to make it right and not worry Mrs. Dority anymore, as she was very concerned for me and my soul. He passed back and forth as he said this, occasionally stopping to look at me and emphasize his point with a shaking finger. He put his hand on my knee, and said he knew I was a good girl and that I had just been lead astray. I rose and said I understood this and would work hard and be good. At this he released me back to my work telling me to be diligent.

As I worked, I was thinking of the unfairness of it, and how morality was to be upheld for some of us, but not for all, (as I knew personally that several of the overseers were entertaining several of the girls after shift). When I arrived back at the boarding house for supper, Mrs. Dority took me aside briefly and told me I could join the other girls, and that I would have a new roommate shortly and that she hoped I had learned a valuable lesson. I said I had, and thanked her for her understanding and that I was sorry for causing her concern. Again I feel like a hypocrite as I don't believe what I say myself. I am more ashamed of lying to people about how I feel, than I am for loving Rebecca.

Wed. Nov. 9, 1898

The girls continue to shun me. I prefer to write from the library where it is not so obvious that no one will sit near me, but I have been reading in the parlor. Whether at the dining table or in the parlor, all the seats near me are abandoned, and they sit cramped together talking in low voices to each other, the furtive glances now replaced by totally ignoring me, as though I don't even exist.

I have picked up several books at the library and quietly read them to shut out the disapproval of the others. Occasionally a girl will shriek with wild laughter, knowing that my concentration on and immersion in my book will be broken. These girls, once so kind, have turned into nasty little agents of morality. I am beginning to hate some of them, especially the ones who seem so bent on meanness. But I maintain my dignified demeanor throughout, which serves only to bring them to new levels of cruelty. One even tripped me as I went down the stairs in the library, and I nearly fell, but caught myself as the books went tumbling, and I thought I could hear giggling as I picked them up from the bottom of the stairs.

Thurs. Nov. 10, 1898

I have received another note, yet still the conveyer is not to be identified. I am told to go to the library and open the Shakespeare tragedy "Romeo and Juliet" to page 57. And so, I have come to the library this evening, and found the volume and bringing it to my table found a letter therein.

It reads, "Dearest D., I am OK. I was given a dishonorable dismissal from the mill. Peter has let a small apartment and we are staying there. It has a back entrance that none can see so that he is not in danger of getting turned out because of having a woman living with him."

"We have decided the best thing to do is to marry. I know this is shocking to you, but please read more to understand what the plan means. If we marry, we can get a larger apartment or a house and you can come to live with us; we can say you are the housekeeper. Peter is getting a promotion and will become, can you believe, an overseer. His larger income will help to support us. You and I can open a small dress shop or do house cleaning to help save for a house in the country where no one knows us. I know you have a small savings, as do I, and all this will go towards our new home. Tell me if you agree with this plan and if so, we can move forward. I hope that you are not suffering too much under the care of Mrs. Dority. I miss you more than you can know. Peter is a gentleman and understands how we want to be with one another. He has a friend whom he also wants to be with but because of circumstances much like ours, he cannot. His friend already lives in the country on a large farm with tenant farmers and Peter thinks that we may be able to stay at one of the vacated tenant's homes and eventually buy it. We could all live there together. I know this is much to digest. I hope you understand and believe that I am trying to do my best to get us back together. Please give me your answer about the plan. With all my Love, R. P.S. Leave your return note in this book at the same page."

I am much thrown by this. Married? Move to the country? It sounds so frightening, so overwhelming, but I miss Rebecca so, that my fears melt away in the face of my passion for her and misery here. I replied, "R., I trust your judgment in this, but I must say it is somewhat startling and sounds farfetched. Yet, I will trust you and follow your lead, simply tell me what I must do. Anything more you can tell me will help put my mind at ease. My heart is in your hands. L., D."

I folded this up and put it in the book, taking the other note and tucking it in my dress, just over my heart.

The library is the fortress wherein I meet my hope and love.

Fri. Nov 11, 1898

I rushed to the library after supper tonight and trying to seem nonchalant while looking about to see if anyone was watching me, I went to the same volume and opened it to the same page. Oh, joy, another note. I unfolded it and read: "Dearest D., I am so overjoyed with your answer. I understand your fears and the unknowns that lie about us like traps, but I trust Peter. I know he will follow through with all he says, and we will be together again sooner than you can imagine. He found he will be able to take the train from the little village where we will soon be living right in to the town not far from the mills. We may be moving directly into the house I mentioned to you. We are going to see it this weekend and I will tell you all about it. We are planning to marry on November 19th either at the town hall or at the house. It would be best if you put in to leave your position now, then you can come for our wedding, and we three will stay in the house. I know this sounds somewhat insane, but I promise you, it will all work out. Do you have the strength to trust me and give notice to the mill? I pray that you do. Stand tight, I will leave another note on Monday. Love, R.

Chapter 29 – Sarah

"Listen, I don't know what happened, but let me explain what's going on in my life." Alice started in without giving me a chance to speak. She stood in the hall holding the bags and gave me an apologetic look.

"Come on in." I took one of the bags and walked ahead of her into the kitchen. "Nothing happened. I just didn't get the job and had to get back to work in Boston," I explained, not being totally truthful.

Alice replied, "Yeah, but without even calling me? Not that I deserve a call, but you just dropped out of sight without even saying goodbye."

"I saw you with that woman and you had your arm around her." As has often happened with me, my mouth led and my brain followed along lamely.

"Oooohhhh, I see." Alice smiled at me, "Let me tell you something you don't know. Can I just make myself at home here?" She said this as she started to unpack one of the bags and take out some rich smelling fresh ground coffee and went with it towards the coffee maker, "Want some coffee? Can I make some?" I nodded yes, and she went about making coffee and talking, as I watched and listened. "I have a really good friend, Laurie, who has been in a relationship with another woman for about five years. I found myself attracted to her lover, but of course, never acted on it. Well they broke up about four months ago and Shirley, Laurie's ex, came to me looking for support. She was depressed and needed a friend. Well, I knew better, I mean after all, it was my good friend she broke up with. I should have listened to my good sense, but she seemed in so much pain. Well, you know what happens sometimes, you have a couple glasses of wine, you try to comfort a crying friend, and pretty soon… well, you know. It was a big, big mistake, and I knew it as soon as we had done it. I think I knew it even before we did it, but I couldn't help myself. So since then, when I see her I end up trying to comfort her and tell her it can't happen again and that I don't feel for her what she wants me to. I don't know what else to do." Alice poured two cups of coffee, handed one to me and took a carton of half and half out of the bag. "So, that's the story, I'm sorry I made a mistake. You saw me trying to confirm that it couldn't happen again, and trying not to hurt her any more than she's already hurting."

I looked at her, sipping the strong, dark coffee. "Sorry, I jumped to a conclusion. I felt hurt. You said you were busy. I didn't understand."

"Listen," Alice smiled at me, but had a serious tone, "I'm not seeing anyone, and haven't been for a while. I had a lover and we broke up about three years ago. It was a hard time and I haven't wanted to get back into any kind relationship again for a while. I guess it goes without saying that I'm a lesbian, did I tell you that? Would it matter? Will you still be my friend?"

"What happened with your girl friend? The one you broke up with?"

"She was cheating on me." She gave me a very serious look. "I guess we'd been drifting apart, different goals or values or something. I wasn't paying enough attention to what was happening with us. Anyway, I didn't find out until it had been going on for a while. That was pretty hard. Imagine the people around you know, your friends know, but they don't tell you, don't think they can tell you, don't think it's their place. Everyone was waiting for her to just leave, but she didn't, she just stayed and continued to cheat. I didn't know. How stupid I was.

"My birthday came along and she didn't show up for dinner, and didn't call home. She'd been staying out late a lot but it didn't dawn on me that anything was up because sometimes she worked late.

"When she finally came home that night, I was still up, and could tell she had been drinking, not drunk, but drinking. I confronted her and she told me to just chill out. I lost my temper. I mean, it was my birthday and she couldn't be there for me? That's when she finally told me. She said she couldn't take it anymore, that she was leaving. It was my damned birthday… Happy Birthday, huh? Well, I found out more details later, but it was over. And that's the story." She took another sip of the coffee and went over to the pot to pour hot coffee into what was rapidly becoming cold coffee. She turned around, leaned against the counter, and looked over at me. "So, what's your story? Or, do you have one?"

"If you're asking me if I'm gay, I don't know, I mean I don't think so, but I did have a crush on a woman in college," I started out, and held my coffee cup out to her to refill. She filled it and I put some cream in. "I was pretty crazy about her, but she wasn't gay, and I fell pretty hard. After that, well, I've dated some guys, but nothing serious, yet. I've thrown myself into my work, some community volunteer work, and I've got some really good friends. I've got acquaintances that go from one failed relationship to another, but not me, sometimes I don't know what I want, or if I want anyone. Not very exciting, huh?"

Alice smiled at me; it was a kind, gentle smile. "It's a true story, and that's all that matters." She crossed the room and gave me a friendly hug. "So, how's the work going here at the house?" She turned back to the bags on the table and started to unpack them. "I hope you don't mind me taking the liberty of picking up a few things, a few groceries, and some stuff most people need when they redecorate or renovate but forget. I got some spackle, a spackle knife, a small pry bar, always handy; and white shellac to cover any stains or paint that might bleed through, a few brushes, and the always popular disposable rubber gloves." She did a little salesman-like flourish as she took each item out of the bag and laid it on the table.

"How did you know I was here?" It just occurred to me how strange it was that after a month of being away, she should just show up on the doorstep with groceries and supplies. She stopped in mid-flourish and looked at me with a sort of apologetic smile.

"Your mother," she said, as though I was supposed to get that. "I told your Mother that if you came back I hoped she would give me a call. She called me yesterday. I like her, she's pretty cool." I felt as though a friendly conspiracy had been formed.

"Really, my Mother called you, and you like her... hmmm, interesting."

"You're not angry, are you?" Alice sounded a little concerned.

"No, I rather like it." I smiled at her.

"Well, as I was saying, what are you working on now, anything that I can help you with?" Alice smiled and started to pore over the lists on the table.

Chapter 30 – Doris

Sat. Nov 12, 1898

I have done it. I have tendered my resignation and asked for my regular discharge papers. So much has happened in this last week I feel as though I no longer know what reality is. By November 19, next Saturday I will be leaving here. I have written Mama and Papa, and tried to put this in the best light, saying I am purchasing this house with my friends from the mill, but I'm fearful they will come after me although I shortly come of age and can refuse to go.

If I can get another placement at a mill, and my hours at the mill were not so rigid, I could also take the train in to work with Peter. Listen to me…I'm talking like this is real, when it all seems so unreal. I only have little pieces of paper saying this is real. I don't know where the house is nor how I will get there, or, if it's all just a bad joke on me.

I go to the book and open it, but I know there will be nothing as she said she would not be able to leave another note until Monday. I smell the pages, imagining I can detect a faint fragrance of Rebecca. What a choice of title, Romeo and Juliet, such a tragedy. My fears are rising again. Perhaps she chose it because of our visit to Norwich to see the play. I hope there is no other meaning and the choice does not portend a tragic future.

Sun. Nov 13, 1898

I have become more and more frightened that this is only a dream. I sit here in my room and read the notes Rebecca has left over and over, trying to see if there is any hidden meaning. I must hide the notes and my journal, fearing Mrs. Dority will again go through the room. I put the notes under my pillow at night and into my dress when I leave for the mill. I put the journal under my mattress, hoping she would not look there. It is such an obvious place, but what else can I do? Mrs. Dority asked me about the resignation, and I told her that I thought it would be best if I tried another mill and another boarding house as the strain of being shunned is taking a toll. She seems to understand this; I will start over, I will do better, I will be a good girl. Mrs. Dority approves. "It is what I have been praying for," she says.

But I myself wonder if I will do better, if I am giving up the only freedom I have ever known, all for something unknown. I don't understand how Peter can be so good and giving and so much of a gentleman. Or, does this give him a hidden pleasure Rebecca doesn't see? Will I indeed be together with Rebecca or will I be but their housekeeper as we are planning to portray, and live a tortured existence forced to witness their wedded bliss? Is Rebecca, as Esther says, untrue and only out to use me? My sanity grows thin with only myself to talk to and work this out with. In less than a week I will know the outcome.

Mon. Nov. 14, 1898

I am here, the volume in front of me and I must now open to page 57 and know if this is my insanity or a shared insanity. There is a note!

"My Dearest, it will not be long until we will be together again. I have seen the house and it is more than I could ever have hoped for. It is a beautiful farmhouse near the big farm. Less than a mile away, there is a small village and depot where the train stops. I think there is also a trolley stop from the depot that goes into the nearest town. There is a flower garden and a big spot for a vegetable garden. We will be able to barter vegetables and eggs in the next year. I am very excited about this. I have taken my savings and given it to Peter. I hope that you can also withdraw yours so that we can give him a good start for the mortgage deposit. I am also hoping you were able to give your notice so that you will be able to come with us on Saturday without the worry of breaking the contract. Please leave note of that in the return note for me. The house is partially furnished so we will have a start on our basic needs without a great outlay. Peter says that his friend from the farm, William, was letting it out to a tenant farmer family that broke the lease and returned to their home state without being able to bring all of their possessions with them. William, being of kind heart let them stay the last month without cost, in exchange for the modest furnishings.

Can you believe this? We are going to have a home! I am so happy! I will leave another note on Wednesday. I love you with all my heart, R."

It becomes more and more real. We are going to do this. I leave my note and pocket Rebecca's. She loves me with all her heart! Dear, dear book, it is real!

Tues. Nov. 15, 1989

It seems that this next week will be the longest of my life. I come back to the library to check the book, still knowing she will not have left another, but yet unable to stop myself from going to this spot, where I know she has been, and touching the book that I know she has touched. The nights are cold and the walks to the library are chilly. I hang by the fireplace in the library, finding comfort in watching the flames licking at the logs, a trancelike state overtakes me and I imagine Rebecca and I back in our bedroom kissing away the chill night air. I try to keep myself calm, try to wait patiently, pushing away the fears. I try to imagine what it will be like. I sometimes wonder if I even want to do this. Is this something which I would have dreamed up, this complex plan? But I am mesmerized by passion, by love.

Wed. Nov. 16, 1898

Yes, there was another note, the day draws nearer and the letter gives me detailed instructions.

"Dearest D., this Friday, you should draw out your savings, and collect your final pay from the mill. Also be sure to get a good letter of recommendation as there is a mill nearby that you may be able to find work at if you choose. See that Mrs. Dority will allow you to stay Friday night if you pay her, even though you will no longer be employed at the mill. Saturday morning there will be a train from your station to Stafford Springs leaving at 7 a.m., but get the ticket only to Merrow as that is where you will get off.

I will meet you at the station there and we can walk back to the house together. We are moving into the house now, and I will not leave any more letters and will not see you until Saturday morning. Don't leave a note as I will not be able to pick it up. We are on our way. I am so very excited I barely can control myself. Peter is almost losing patience with my excitement. We will be wed at the house by a local justice. We will have only us few, you, William, Peter, the justice and I. Hold strong and steady in our plans. Love, R."

Thurs. Nov. 17, 1898

It is cold but I went out to walk tonight, I could not stay still. I am back now in the parlor, sitting as close to the fire as possible with the other girls sitting nearer, and no one willing to let me in. I will not need to endure this behavior much longer. I find it hard to sleep, what with the excitement and ideas racing through my mind at night. I dream of a white farm house, of dancing with Rebecca in the garden, of holding her close in our bed with no fear of Mrs. Dority throwing the door open. Then I think of Peter and wonder what difficulty he may impose upon us. I try to sleep, I count numbers to try to become drowsy, but my mind wanders back to the events of this past week. I try not to think of these events and try to count again. Oh please, blessed sleep, embrace me.

Fri. Nov. 18, 1898

I have been busily tying up the loose ends. Mrs. Dority will let me stay the night. I have packed my few things and have laid out an outfit for tomorrow. It is done. I have my regular discharge and my savings; I am ready. I am finally tired, with all the packing and work to get it all finished. What if this is a hoax? What if she is not there? What if I am treated poorly? What will I do, where will I go? I cannot go home. Should I save a small amount to escape with enough to catch a train to the city? I must quiet my mind, and hopefully I will sleep tonight.

Chapter 31 – Sarah

The next day I woke stiff and worn out, before I even got out of bed. I stumbled down the stairs and made some coffee, grateful for the pound that Alice had brought. While I was toasting a bagel, I started to run a bath into the big claw-foot tub. I didn't have the time for a long bath ritual, but felt like I needed a little soak just to get the stiffness out from work on the previous day. I found some Epsom salts in the almost barren linen closet and ran the water very hot while I sat on the edge crunching through the bagel and sipping the coffee. My toes were rebelling against the hot water as I eased myself in and leaned back. My back was shocked by the cold of the cast iron as it gradually came up to temperature. I took a deep breath, let out a big sigh, and thought I heard a faint knock at the door. I waited, listening, wondering if it was just pipes expanding after months without use. Again, I heard knocks, this time louder.

"Hold on a minute, I'll be right there." I hollered, jumping out and doing a quick wipe down and tossing on my robe.

At the door, Harry, looking shy and almost ready to flee, thrust a bag overflowing with bacon, milk, bread, eggs and cheese into my arms.

"Hi, Bea said you would be here and I had a light workload this morning, so I hoped you wouldn't mind if I came over and offered a hand."

"No, of course not, come on in." Thinking Bea was indeed a busy bee, I showed him through the parlors to the kitchen in the back, offered him some coffee and excused myself to dress.

While I was upstairs, I could hear Harry rustling in the kitchen and banging around a little, and as I combed my hair, the enticing aroma of bacon wafted up the stairs. I could only think that I was very lucky to have such thoughtful and easygoing friends who felt they could walk into my house and start cooking. Maybe I should have felt it was an affront to my culinary capabilities, but instead I felt fortunate.

I came down to find a plate of bacon and eggs; the eggs were crisp at the edges but still looked good enough to eat. Harry turned around and gave me a sad little puppy dog look. "I'm sorry, I burned the eggs. I couldn't find a spatula and had to use a butter knife." He pushed the plate towards me and scooped out the rest onto a plate for himself.

"I hope you don't mind me making myself at home. I thought you might want a good breakfast after all your work here and this kitchen is so similar to mine, it just invited me in to cook." He gave me a crooked smile as he wiped a little grease from his chin.

"Oh, no, this is great." Thinking, everyone seems to be doing that these days, but I restrained myself from saying that.

We talked a little about my plans to fix up the old place. He talked about vet work in a small town, and how, once people know your work, animals seem to flow your way. Then he talked about his father and grandfather.

"My Dad is a funny old coot; he's got his ways about him that are never going to change. For some reason, he just sort of turned against my granddad. Maybe it was just the generational thing that he never grew out of, I don't know. But he didn't like Peter, your granddad either, or Becky or Aunt Doris. He never said much about it, but when I was a kid and Peter and Becky would stop over, he would find a way to get busy and avoid spending time with them. He was fine with the other neighbors who had bought all the old tenant farms, but he seemed to have a *thing* about Pete and Becky, and even Bea. It was too bad, because I would have liked to get to know them. But I ended up in the largest tenant farm, out near the main road, and set up my practice there and it's worked out well. Charlie, my younger brother, runs the farm with his kids and I help them when they need vet care. I'm pretty happy here, and it's nice to know a younger person, a relative of Pete and Becky, is buying the old place and giving it some attention." I watched his long fingers move about expressively as he talked and I ate the burnt eggs. "So, I'm doing all the talking, tell me about yourself, what brings you back here?"

"I'm not sure what brings me back, maybe it's the roots thing, maybe it's the pace, the simplicity; maybe it's a good deal. But for right now, it seems like the right thing."

"Well, I hear you're a, uh compositor, and Bea is an accountant; but what about your grandparents? Tell me about them. I only know what little gossip I get through town, and it seems they were pretty modest."

"Oh," I started hedging, not sure how much I could or wanted to tell him. "Well, um, I didn't know them very well. I know Pete liked to garden, that he worked at one of the mills and that in their younger years, Becky and Aunt Doris did, too. That is where they all met."

"And that's it?"

"Well, I'm learning more as I clean out the house. If I come across any revelations, I'll keep you posted."

"Well, I'm glad you're more sociable than some of the other people around; small town life can be strange. People seem to know everything about you and yet not know you at all. And as an eligible bachelor in town, mothers seem to be pretty pushy." At that he glanced at me, flustered and blushing. "Oh, I didn't mean… sorry, I didn't mean you and Bea."

"That's OK. Well, thanks for the breakfast; that was sweet. Let me take care of these dishes, OK?" I said, quickly changing the subject, which seemed to relieve him. I scooped up dishes and mugs and put them all in the sink. "So, this is my to-do list. How are you at spackling and sanding? I'm hoping to get a coat of paint on the bathroom tomorrow if I can get it spackled today." Harry looked at the list, nodded and said he was up to the task.

Chapter 32 – Doris

Sat. Nov 19, 1898

I am on my way, but the devil only knows where to. The motion of the train rocking side to side is comforting and solid-feeling, but I am a jumble of nerves. It is a chilled morning and the day is barely dawned. A kind man helped me get my band box and carpet bag onto the train, and I found a seat as close to the door as possible as I cannot easily carry all of this by myself. The town is a distant scene that the train draws away from; the tall spires of the churches, the large mill buildings, the smaller homes on the hills, all are becoming smaller and smaller. The tracks follow the river that feeds the mill, a fine and powerful river with strong falls and pretty pools. Now we're passing farms and small villages. At each village the whistle blows and sometimes we stop for a few minutes and one or two people come into the car. Now and again we pass through a wooded area. More farms, more woods, another small village, then, finally, the whistle blows and the conductor cries, "Merrow". I must pack up my dear book. Oh, I see her; she's at the platform waving. Oh, my dear heart!

Mon. Nov 21, 1898

How can I possibly remember and collect all my thoughts? These last few days have been a whirlwind of excitement and change and joy; finally, joy. Dear book, I write you now from my room, my own room! Saturday morning, Rebecca was there at the station, as she said she would be. She helped me carry my bag and band box; we had only to go perhaps a mile up from the station, and even with the bare branches it was still pretty. But everything looks pretty now that we are together again. Once out of sight of the small station and other houses, she stopped, put my bag down and hugged and kissed me, holding me so tightly, and I her. Going on a little further, where another road intersects, was a lovely house which is to be our home. We put my things upstairs in what Rebecca said was to be my room, which was off the hall, but also attached by a door to her room.

We went downstairs to find Peter and William in the kitchen carving a cooling roast that we were to have for dinner. Rebecca pitched right in and started boiling potatoes and carrots for the feast. Peter introduced me to William, the gentleman farmer from the adjoining farm who is to be selling us this home. He is a pleasant and quiet gentleman.

Peter took me aside, into the front parlor. From his vest he drew a small ring; he asked for my hand, and taking it he slipped the ring onto my little finger. It was a plain band. He held my hand and said to trust him; and not to worry and that he was very happy that I had arrived safely and that we would be living together. All this surprised and confused me, I pulled my hand away, and went to take the ring off, but he touched my hand and said no, please don't, it will all be clear soon, and it will be to your satisfaction. I just looked at him and said thank you. I could find no other words as I was so confused.

Then, Rebecca beckoned to us from the kitchen. Peter took my hand and led me back. Rebecca gave me an apron and had me start to clean up a pumpkin for a pie. We were all busy in the kitchen, and the talk was of the weather and the justice who would be arriving in several hours to marry Peter and Rebecca. The kitchen stove, a plain Kenwood, was stoked and made the kitchen very warm. I was so confused and hungry and close to fainting. I sat down at the table, put my head in my hands and started to cry. Everyone stopped and looked over at me. Then, they all came over and Rebecca put her arms around me and said I was a poor thing, and had gone through so much lately. "Peter, give me your handkerchief," she said. "And get her some water. William, please get her something to eat, she probably hasn't had anything since supper yesterday." Rebecca dried my tears and gave me water. William sliced some thin bits of the roast and buttered a piece of bread and put the meat on it and offered it to me. Everyone was so kind to me, I cried even more as I ate and drank. But shortly some tea fortified me, and soon I was laughing with them about the strange little justice they were expecting.

Once we had most of the kitchen work done, I helped set the table with the nice linens and china that William had brought over to celebrate the occasion.

Justice Lairdly arrived and he was as unusual as they had described: short and bald with thick eyeglasses, and a large handlebar moustache. He looked much like a gnome, but he was professional and not only would he do their rites, but was also going to photograph them. With a flourish he produced a compact device that unfolded to support a camera. We were directed to assemble in the front parlor, while Justice Lairdly set up the camera. Then, with Peter and Rebecca together and William next to Peter, and I next to Rebecca, he said a very simple wedding rite. Peter placed a ring on Rebecca's hand, much like he had on mine, kissed her gently on the forehead and Justice Lairdly declared them married and we all signed the marriage certificate.

Then, we all stood very still in the places he had assigned to us and looked at the camera while he took the picture. He folded up the camera, wished Peter and Rebecca well, and told us he would be back with the picture in 3 weeks. We waved as he briskly went out, packed his buggy, pulled the blanket off of his horse and drove away. And that is how Peter and Rebecca were married. We all returned to the kitchen and served ourselves up a sumptuous supper. William produced a large bottle of wine and for the first time, I had a glass of wine. I did not care for the taste much, but it did get refilled a second time, and it left me feeling very silly. William toasted Peter and Rebecca, Peter toasted Rebecca and me, Rebecca toasted Peter and William and when they looked to me, I smiled and toasted us all; then we all got to laughing.

I had been so fearful of the event, not understanding why or how, just trusting that it would work out and Rebecca and I would be together, and here we were. They were married and we were all eating and drinking and laughing in our own home, or what would soon be our own home. I still found it impossible to believe and understand, but stopped trying after my third glass of wine when I grew very silly indeed. After Rebecca said I must be tired and we should retire, Peter and William went into the parlor and smoked cigars, while Rebecca and I cleared the table. Rebecca led me up the stairs while the men continued to smoke and talk and laugh, and I think, have more wine.

She led me to her room, where she made me stand before her, and give her my hand. I was so silly that she had difficulty getting me to understand, as she said to me, "Here, now, you must be serious and give me your hand." She took my hand and removed my ring and put it into my palm, then she took off her ring and holding my hand she said, "With this ring, I Thee Wed" and put her ring onto my finger. She placed her hand in mine and motioned for me to do the same. This brought me to my senses somewhat, and I took the ring and gently slid it onto her finger, looking intently at that hand, at the ring, and hesitantly whispered the words she had said, "With this ring, I Doris Biracree, wed thee, Rebecca Moorhouse." As I looked into her smiling eyes, we both suddenly fell somber; this was the impossible made possible. Both of us were filled with the joy and satisfaction that we had arranged to be together again, only this time, forever. There was a small cloud of discomfort and nervousness too. She blew out the candle, then kissed my neck, then my shoulder as she started to undress me, and I her. All that I had ever dreamt of filled the rest of our night together.

It never occurred to me that she should be spending her wedding night with Peter or that she would ever spend a night with Peter. Not on that night it didn't.

Chapter 33 – Sarah

Alice came by in the afternoon and proved that she was very clever at renovating; as I went over the plans she understood exactly what I was trying to do, and was able to make helpful suggestions for execution and cost-cutting. We spent so much time going over the plans, measuring this, and sketching that, we ended up going out to dinner rather than starting any projects.

We talked some more about the house and about other things; including relationships, parents and work. Alice had gone to college and majored in business and marketing but found the field stressful, especially for women. The other classmates, mostly men, were mean and treated her with contempt, or worse, ignored her as though she didn't exist. When a friend offered her a part- time job at the garage for fun, she found she liked it so much, she ended up quitting school in her junior year and started working at the garage full-time. I liked that she was more interested in honoring her values and happiness than in struggling up a difficult business ladder.

We had a few beers and the daily special at the local greasy spoon and when she dropped me off she offered to come by the next day after work to give me a hand.

I welcomed all her help. We hugged goodbye and I went to my new house planning to work myself until I was exhausted.

The next morning found me in bed, still in my work clothes, with a blanket pulled over me. I got up, made some coffee and decided to start in the bathroom with a coat of primer on the trim, ceiling and walls. I was going to leave the old floor which was done in those tiny octagonal black and white tiles. It was a good look with the old tub and I was thinking about getting an old-fashioned-looking toilet. I had even picked out a new medicine cabinet with an oval mirror that added to the old- fashioned charm. I was excited about how nice it was going to be.

Bea showed up around lunchtime with good coleslaw and fried chicken in a bucket that I really appreciated after my morning of painting and errands. She left by 4:00 and neither of us mentioned Alice or Harry. I thought she gave me a few sideways glances, but I chose to ignore them. I was sure she was dying to talk about both of them, but the fun of making her wait was too much to pass up.

Alice came over around 5:00 and we surveyed the yard and my plans there. The yard dropped off in the back to the south and then leveled out into what would be a perfect vegetable garden. I think Pete had grown vegetables there at one point, but as he got older it was hard for him to make the trip up and down the steep hill so they were moved up to the side yard. There was a beautiful clump of lilacs anchoring the southeast corner of it with a little stone bench under it. We were talking about all these plans when Alice said, "You've got to take a break. You can't work like this day in and day out; it's not good for you. When is your appointment?"

"At the paper? Tomorrow morning."

"OK, then will you go out for a walk with me tomorrow afternoon? I've got a place I'd like you to see."

"I'd love to go for a walk, but I've got so much…"

I started to look for excuses when Alice interrupted, "Good. Tomorrow afternoon, I'll pick you up; say around 1:00, is that late enough? You'll be back from the appointment by then, right?"

"OK, yes." I was still sounding hesitant.

"See, that wasn't hard, you can take time to relax some. You're going to love this place. It's got local lore and legend, old stories circulated about it. And by the way, good luck tomorrow."

"Yeah, OK, thanks."

Chapter 34 – Doris

Tues. Nov 22, 1898

I sit at my desk again, still adjusting to the incredible events of the past few weeks. Just over two weeks ago we were blissfully passing our time at the boarding house. Working, socializing, and meeting in the evenings in our bedroom. Now we live together in our spacious and comfortable home. I must soon find a job though, as I feel I must contribute more to our household. William says the local mill, which is small, is often looking for good workers and with my experience I will likely be able to get a position without difficulty. I can walk to the railroad station which can take me to Willington, where the mill is. Rebecca makes sandwiches and coffee and sends these with Peter in the morning. He started back to work already. We are a happy little household and neighbors would have no idea what arrangements have been made here. I must wonder about Peter, he seems kind and content, but I don't fully understand his business here with us. Why would a man not take a wife as most men do? I know there is a close bond between him and William and I wonder if it is of the same nature as Rebecca and me. That would be a strange coincidence, or perhaps there is more to the mystery that I don't know of.

Thur. Nov 24, 1898

I visited the Willington mill and applied for a job and met the agent there who thinks he could find a place for me almost immediately. He said that I should return on Monday, ready to start a new job. This company works with cotton thread, and ships to a large distribution company. Days grow shorter and I am grateful that my room is over the kitchen, for when I write it keeps me warm, but my evenings are spent in Rebecca's room where I have no need for more warmth.

Sat. Nov. 26, 1898

We will be having a roast tomorrow, and Rebecca and I went to the market for the trimmings. William has been generous with several bushels of potatoes and carrots which we've stored in the cellar, but we are in need of flour and sugar and tea. William will be over for Sunday supper, as he often is, and we welcome him, such a fine and gentle man.

Mon. Nov. 28, 1898

I have started my new job as an operative at the mill. I think I will fit in well there. Rebecca now makes lunches for both Peter and I, and this morning left a little note in mine which I was fearful someone would find, so I tucked it carefully away after I read it. How dear and joyous my life is now.

Tues. Nov. 29, 1898

I have a received a letter from Abigail who said that Mama and Papa want to come and visit my new home. I wonder how I will be able to present this to them. They are hoping to come in several weeks. It will only be for a Sunday, so we will not need to be concerned about how to bed everyone, but still I am nervous at the prospect.

Wed. Nov 30, 1898

We are planning to have a late Thanksgiving dinner tomorrow. Of course, William will be our primary guest. Peter has gotten a turkey and we are busy making pies tonight and preparing for this big meal. I am so tired I can barely write.

Sun. Dec 4, 1898

What a wonderful meal we cooked and again, William brought several bottles of wine and we ate and drank and laughed until everyone was full and tired. Rebecca and I cleaned up while Peter and William went for a walk and we retired before they returned. I suspect they go to William's house on these evening jaunts. I am so happy here, happy with our life together, happy to just have a simple life with Becky, it is all so perfect. Is this a dream that I will wake from? Why am I so fearful?

Chapter 35 – Sarah

Excited about the interview, I got up early. I showered in the old tub, grateful for the new shower curtain, and that Bea had taken the time to do such a good job cleaning the tub.

I dressed in a comfortable but professional-looking outfit and headed out to the second interview at the paper. It was, as I had remembered, a perfect fit. I could really get into working there, having such an easy commute and being in this small community. I suppose a small community has its drawbacks, but it also gives you a sense of belonging that is often missing in a city.

I was happy that, rather than keeping me in suspense, they offered me the job, then and there. The salary was acceptable considering my experience so I didn't play any games, I just accepted the offer. There was much handshaking all around and an offer to do lunch. I told them I could do a very early lunch but that I had to leave by noon, we ended up deciding on a rain check. I was to start in two weeks, which was perfect. I could spend some time working on the house and then put in a final week at my old job. I felt a pang of regret over my old job, but everything else was so right I knew that I had to make the leap.

I drove home, changed my clothes for my walk with Alice, and called my old job to give them a verbal notice that I was expecting to leave in a couple of weeks. I knew there were apprentice advertising assistants and experienced compositors waiting in the wings to step into a position like the one I was moving from, so I didn't feel as though I was leaving them in a bind.

While I was on the phone, Alice knocked and came in, bringing a loaf of bread, peanut butter, jelly and bananas. She busied herself making sandwiches while I finished up the phone call.

"How about some coffee?" I said as I got off the phone and started to set up the coffeemaker. "I sure could use some."

"OK, one sandwich or two?"

"One is fine," I said as we both sat down to sandwiches with a banana on the side.

Once we were on our way in Alice's truck, she pointed out some of the sights I'd never noticed or knew about. We went through Willimantic, where Rebecca, Doris and Peter all met, then on further until we got to Baltic, where we parked on the outskirts of town.

As we started our walk, Alice introduced me to our surroundings. "This was another textile mill town, like so many towns in New England. With plenty of waterfalls, these little villages depended on the mills, which depended upon the water to drive the machines. Of course these towns needed a ready supply of workers and usually built row houses and duplexes to house families close to the mill."

She paused to open the gate and let me through, and went on, "Sometimes they also had boarding houses where they could put up single people. Well, there is a legend about this town, about a group of women who lived in the woods, down this dirt road. And these women entertained, *and you know what I mean by entertained*, the mill boys. In return the mill boys would bring them what they needed to live on: food, beer, wood, kerosene, sometimes clothes, or fineries and a little money. The women moved there because they had nowhere else to go. They were outcasts and they bonded together to help each other and made a living the only way they knew how. Some of the larger towns had poor houses where destitute people lived. Some destitute people were taken in by their families, but some alcoholics or maladjusted people were outcast and became vagrants or thieves. These women were just getting along the best they could."

Alice told this story as we walked along the dirt road through some fields and along by the river that feeds the mill below. "Anyway, the story goes that amongst these women were two lesbians. And they agreed to entertain the boys as long as when it was time to go to sleep for the evening, they could sleep together, alone. The madam agreed and they were living up here together for years." She paused to climb down to the river and look at it. A pretty waterfall and large pool gave way to more waterfalls. The pool rippled with the movement of fish and flowering bushes scented the air.

"The madam's name was Jenny and the road to the little camp was called Jenny's Way. Well, as it happens, the town turned on the women, Jenny died and after a while, everyone got assimilated back into the town. And that's the short version of the story."

We walked further on, and gradually the road turned and rose up a hill. Not too far up the hill there were broken down shacks, not much left really, rotted wood, old wire bedsprings, an old rusted metal barrel, a few bottles. But you could imagine it. You could feel the history come alive.

I said to Alice, "You're right; there is something special about this. And it makes me think of the history of it, and the history of all of us and our parents and grandparents and heritage, all that has come before us. The history that people want to hide, that often is successfully hidden, and lost. Thanks for taking me here."

"Yeah, I often wonder about all the lost stories, the lost histories of gay people. You know, there have been gay people since there were people, but you never hear about them. They have always been invisible, probably because it was the only way they could survive. But it's sad, and I'm glad you're going to preserve those journals of your grandmother and her lover. We are here, we are real and no matter how much society protests and tries to hush us, we will still survive, and some of our stories will too."

"I agree, but, I'm still not sure if I am one of you." Something militant and insistent about Alice scared me. I wasn't sure I was a lesbian. I wasn't sure what I felt for anyone of either sex. When I had that college crush, it was like an obsession, something I felt I couldn't control. I didn't think I felt that way about Alice. I haven't felt that way about anyone since. And the idea of it was distressing. I bought into society's model of the norm and wasn't sure I wanted to pay the price of being different.

Alice gave me a long look, then said, "Why, because you haven't felt the obsession you did when you were in college?" She understood, and I nodded. We walked back down the dirt road in silence, both immersed in our own thoughts.

Chapter 36 – Doris

Mon. Dec 5, 1898

I had started to feel so comfortable, so much like my life was perfect, but it was a foolish imagining. Last evening Becky told me what I was fearful of all along, fearful of without even knowing it. She said there had been an agreement made, before we came to live together, an agreement between her and Peter that if we were to be successful in the plans to marry and buy the house, that he would want to have children.

"What does that mean?" I asked, dumbfounded, knowing exactly what it meant and dreading it. "Why didn't you tell me this before?" She replied that she feared I wouldn't come if she told me, and she was probably right. I had to sit there for a while to take all of this in. "When?" I said. "Soon," she said. I was shaken to my very core. What would happen, would she leave me, would she stay with Peter and not be mine anymore? Had she been with him before? I was assaulted with fears, and every way I examined it, I could see no good outcome for me. Rebecca could see the pain on my face and tried to comfort me, but I pushed her away, feeling betrayed, saying "Esther warned me, but I wouldn't listen." Rebecca turned and went downstairs, I heard her talking to Peter, quietly, and then I heard them moving about and the door closing. This upset me even more. I ran down the stairs, almost falling in my haste and threw open the door, only to see them bundled up, walking away. I closed the door and paced around the house, around through the parlors, into the kitchen, down the back hall to the front door, and then back through the parlors, faster and faster, around and around, my mind spinning. What am I to do? Why did I say that to Rebecca? Then a knock came at the door. William came in. He hugged me, took my arm and led me into the kitchen where he sat me down at the table. As I watched him, he went through the cupboards and came out with two glasses and a bottle. He poured two small amounts of what I believe was brandy into the glasses and handed one to me. "You know, Doris," he began, "Rebecca loves you very much and that will never change. You should not fear losing Rebecca." He sipped his drink and motioned for me to sip mine. I did and he continued, "For us to live in this little town with these wagging tongues, we need to seem like a family, like regular people or those righteous ones will drive us out of town. Do you know that?" I nodded, feeling a little better. William, with all his common sense and his gentle voice, calmed me. I felt I'd been close to going mad. He kept talking and refilling our glasses. "Doris, you are a fine woman and we are going to have a fine family, the four of us." I looked at him. He asked me about the new job at the mill and how I liked it. He asked me if I knew how to garden and if I enjoyed it, and if could I grow a good Brussels sprout. He asked me about my parents and about my hometown. We talked until it became very late and both of us a little tipsy. He persuaded me to retire and as I was readying for bed, I heard the door open and voices drifted up the stairway. Rebecca came upstairs and readied for bed as always, and climbed in with me. She put her arms around me and held me and kissed my forehead and said she loved me and I should not worry, and we fell asleep.

Tues. Dec. 6, 1898

Work helps to bring me to reality. So much seems like a dream in these last few months, but work is good and solid. I am in our room and after supper Rebecca sits on our bed and mends a blouse for me. I look over and she smiles that beautiful smile. We haven't talked of last night and I don't know if we will. She is being very kind to me, and I to her. Peter reads his paper or visits William. I am grateful to William who I understand now to be a true friend and good man.

Thurs. Dec. 8, 1898

Life is settled down. We are planning for Mama and Papa's visit next month. Maybe Abigail will come with them. I don't think I realized how much I missed them until I found they planned to visit. We have two spare small rooms, one which has a single bed. We think that my Mother and Father can bed in my room and Abigail in the extra room. I can sleep in Rebecca's room and Rebecca can sleep with Peter. The thought of them together again puts that old fear in me, but it is only for my parents that we would do this, I am assured.

Sat. Dec. 10, 1898

It grows cold and snows now. Our walk to the train station will be harder. On occasion we may be able to catch a ride with a delivery man whose rounds bring him by very early. We are busy cleaning out the root cellar so that we will be able to store our garden's produce next fall. It is a little stone room that can be reached from the cellar, cold and damp, but with a little airflow that will keep the stored vegetables well. We plan our garden. William has given us some seeds he has saved from his garden, so we will have a fine planting in the spring. We will get our coal delivery next week so we will be able to keep warm during the holidays.

Chapter 37 – Sarah

Everyone was pleased that I got the new job, but I knew that it meant I would need to work hard to get the house fairly comfortable before I had to go back to Boston. So when I went to the store I got all I thought I'd need to finish this first phase: faucet parts for the kitchen, a little more paint, and other odds and ends. Alice installed the new light fixture and medicine chest in the bath. I finished painting the trim and put some lacy curtains up that fit the style of the room perfectly. A small old-fashioned vanity chair finished off the whole effect. We did a great job, and it was charming. I wondered what Rebecca and Doris would think if they were to come back and see this.

Now I had to go back to Boston, finish up my old job, pack up my belongings and move them down. Alice wanted to help with moving, and Harry did too, but I thought I could do most of the packing and moving down myself. Betsy and Maureen would probably help and they had a van so that would carry a fair amount. I thought Alice and Harry could help when I arrived.

I went back to Boston and busied myself packing in the evenings after work. Betsy and Maureen had me over for dinner on the Friday evening before I was to move. They would be helping me in the morning. We talked of our friendships, and how they would miss having me in such close proximity. I assured them I wasn't that far away and that they could visit me in the country whenever they wanted to, and that I would definitely visit them. Talk then turned to the house and the journals, and finally I felt I needed to tell them about Alice and Harry, before they arrived to find the attractive mechanic and veterinarian working in my house.

"Well, another thing I've been meaning to tell you, I have some friends in Connecticut." They both turned towards me at the same time, eyebrows raised expectantly.

"Some friends?" they said in unison. "I thought you said you didn't have anyone?" Betsy was reminding me of our conversation.

"You two are so cute. Yes, I have some new friends, and they'll probably be around helping me move in, I don't want you to be taking me aside while they are there, so ask any questions you have now."

"So, tell us more. Women? Men? Names? Come on, don't be so vague, and fill us in." The barrage of questions started.

"Well, first of all, nothing is going on. A woman named Alice, she's fun, and you'll like her, but don't be pairing us up, OK? She's a mechanic."

"A mechanic? Cool. Tell us more."

"Well, she went to school for business and marketing, but found it too stressful, so she went to work for a friend who has a garage. She fixed my flat tire the first day I was down there, that's about it." I knew this could cause some questions.

"You didn't tell us anything about her."

"She's nice; she hasn't been in a relationship for a while and like me, isn't looking for one. She's been helping me with the renovations. She's pretty good at that stuff and I'm learning a lot from her."

"And the other friend is a man, his name is Harry, he's a vet and lives down the road a short way. He grew up there right next door to my grandparents; he's easygoing and intense all at the same time. I like him, but I don't have any plans with either of them. OK, you got it?"

"Really, he grew up there? Do you think he knows anything about the goings on at your grandparents? I mean, they must have tried to keep it a secret." Maureen was wondering, as was I, about how the town tolerated the family, or if they ever figured it out.

"I don't know yet, but Harry did say that his father avoided our family, so he might have known, or suspected something."

I went home early that evening to get some rest for the big moving day tomorrow.

The next day I got up early, had my coffee and a large bowl of cereal, and then started packing my car. I really didn't have too much stuff for someone who lived in this apartment for the last five years. With careful packing, I thought we could do it all in one trip. Some kitchen stuff, a few favorite bowls and good pans, basic small appliances, linens and a few pieces of furniture.

The big stuff could fit into the van first, and then pack everything else around it. Anything I left behind was Betsy and Maureen's to keep or give away. They agreed that anything they didn't want would go to Goodwill.

My car was packed by the time Betsy and Maureen arrived. With their help it went quickly and we had the van packed in no time, and we were on our way out of town before noon.

When we arrived at the house Betsy and Maureen got out and marveled at it. It was beautiful, they said, just beautiful. I knew it needed work and pointed out the broken porch railing and peeling paint and miscellaneous things, but they knew the value of a sound home, a lovely home in the country. We had stopped for grinders near the house and decided to eat before we started to unpack. While we were sitting in the kitchen, someone knocked at the door and came in. It was Bea.

"Hey, ya! How are you girls doing?" Bea had met Betsy and Maureen before and liked them. Bea had strong likes and dislikes, and she knew what she felt, so I was always happy when she liked my friends. She went over and gave each of them a hug. "So, what do you think of my little girl? She bought her grandmother's old place, and is doing a damned fine job of fixing it up, too." No modesty there, Bea just glowed as she spoke.

"We think it's wonderful, we're very excited about it," Betsy was enthusiastic.

Bea sidled over to Maureen and jabbed her in the ribs "And what about that friend of hers, she's quite a looker, huh? And the vet's pretty cute, too." I just looked from her to them and back to her, shaking my head, mouth open, mortified. They all started to laugh.

"Ma, if you're referring to Alice and Harry, they haven't even met them yet."

"Oh? Well, you will. I'm sure she'll be here any minute." And right on cue, there was a knock at the door. "Come on in." Bea hollered.

Alice came in, tall and handsome; her long, straight, dark brown hair was pulled back at the nape of her neck. She was wearing a white blouse with the top two buttons unbuttoned, and her nice-fitting jeans with boots. Her lips… My God, I thought, she's gorgeous, and then quickly thought what am I thinking? Alice greeted Bea with a European air kiss on the cheek and then did the same to me.

"Hi, I'm Alice," extending her hand to Betsy, who looked flustered, but shook Alice's hand.

"Hi, I'm Betsy, and this is, um, Maureen," Betsy faltered as Maureen put out her hand. "Hi." Maureen said. I looked from Betsy to Maureen. Both were mesmerized with Alice. I had to admit, she never looked so good.

"Well," Alice started right in, "What can I help with? You haven't gotten it all moved in yet, have you?"

"No, no, no, we're just breaking for lunch after the drive out. You're just in time." Thankful that Alice had broken the spell, I offered her a grinder.

Another knock at the door and Harry walked in, muck boots, flannel shirt, hair tousled, looking ever like the country vet. I was getting more frazzled by the minute. Bea did the introductions. Alice and Harry smiled, and did the cursory I-think-I've-seen-you-around-town talk, but I thought I felt a little tension there.

Betsy and Maureen, just kept looking from one to the other and to me, smiling politely, but I could see the wheels furiously turning.

Talk was light and varied, about Boston, women mechanics, veterinary duties and of course, renovations. Then we got down to moving everything in and I was able to direct a lot of the boxes into the rooms where they would be needed. Some things I just had them put in Pete's room, which was the most convenient, since it was so close to the front door. This way I could work on a room, finish it, and take my time moving things into place.

I was finally moving in, my home, my roots, and a whole new life.

Chapter 38 – Doris

Tues. Dec. 13, 1898

We have made our rooms plain enough that one can barely discern who is living in which room except for the clothes. We thought this could be explained away as Rebecca having too little room in Peter's closet, so each person has their own. We also thought it would seem funny if my room adjoined Rebecca's, so we made the marriage bed appear to be in Peter's room by adding a few of Rebecca's personal items. It seems dishonest and petty to stoop to this kind of deception, but it will put my family at ease. I cannot imagine the response if they were to discover the nature of our relationship and I can only base it on the reaction from Mrs. Dority. Personally, I am happy not to have to change my room too much except to put my journal and a few personal letters away.

Sun. Dec. 18, 1898

My Mama and Papa and little Abigail have visited and left.

Little Abigail has grown so. We had William to our house for dinner with my family so that it was a large and busy affair with all the women in the kitchen while the men went walking. William showed Papa his farm. I know that this has both parents believing there will be an alliance between William and me and I am not discouraging this right now as it will help to make them feel this is a good spot for me to alight. It was very good to see them, but my life has changed so much since then. I feel I have left the little innocent hamlet of my youth behind and written onto the slate of my history. I cannot imagine returning to it and the simple life I once led.

Sun. Dec. 25, 1898

We had a quiet Christmas Eve dinner, just the four of us. The bustle of the last few months is behind us and we're all hoping for a quieter year ahead. Our Christmas was simple and modest; gifts were exchanged, Peter gave me a bottle of ink which I needed and Rebecca gave me a lovely night gown. William surprised us all with a new settee and our parlor is looking more and more comfortable.

Mon. Dec. 26, 1898

We are all discouraged as we are sure now that Rebecca does not carry a child. There is talk of another attempt, but little is said in my presence. I am becoming more comfortable with it as Rebecca did indeed return to my bed and shows me without reserve her love and passion. Little endearments pass from her lips, whispered into my ears often during the most mundane of evenings while we are at the sink or reading in the small parlor.

Sun. Jan 1, 1899

Rebecca went to Peter's bed again last night. William came to visit us and after dinner walked me over to his house. A fine Christmas tree was still set up in the parlor. His housekeeper bustled about settling me into a comfortable chair by the fire, bringing a lap robe for me, and brandy for both William and me. William talked of the crops he would be planting and the pigs and cows he expected to have in the spring. He also mentioned that a fox had carried away several of his chickens. The farm is a passion for him and it is apparent how dearly he holds it and enjoys managing and working it. His tenant farmers help to run the farm and the biggest adversity, he says, is due to the vagaries of the weather. It was actually a pleasant evening and I would have fully enjoyed it if I hadn't known the reason for my visit. He asked about my job and if I still liked it, and I told him I do like it well enough. When the clock struck 9:00, he rose and said we should get me back home. I bundled up again and he walked me back. When I went up into Rebecca's room she was already there, waiting for me as though nothing were different. Her ardor was just the same.

Tues Jan. 24, 1899

The snow is such that both Peter and I are having difficulty getting to the train station. William has come down with a cutter and horse several times to help us. I fear for my job if I miss time, but so far we have managed to get there.

Sat. Feb. 11, 1899

We think that Rebecca will have a baby, as she has become somewhat sick in the morning. Her appetite grows stronger once she feels better, later in the day. Peter is looking very cheerful and Rebecca too, when she is not feeling sickly. We all watch and worry and fuss over her, bringing her treats when she has a yearning for something. Even though she tells us not to go to the trouble, we can see the pleasure she derives from so much attention and we enjoy finding ways to spoil her.

Sun. Feb. 12, 1899

Rebecca slept late this morning and I made breakfast. She thinks that just being around the smell of the eggs contributes to her feeing poorly. Excitement over her pregnancy is growing. William came over to breakfast with a big smoked ham for us to have and we are looking forward to the nice dinner that it will provide. We were disappointed that Rebecca didn't come down to join us, but we were still quite a jovial group.

Sun. Mar. 19, 1899

Oh, it was such a sad day. Rebecca had taken to the bed not feeling well. While she was there, the baby came, dead. We are all sad, and can but only grieve for Rebecca and the tiny thing barely bigger than a peanut. Peter came in and brought warm, wet cloths and waited downstairs while I washed Rebecca. After, Rebecca washed the tiny, frail little body then she tucked it in a soft flannel pocket so that we could prepare it to be buried. Peter built a tiny coffin and we all went down to the back garden where he had dug a hole beneath the still leafless lilac. We all fussed over the burial site for a few minutes, I put a few Johnny-Jump-Up seeds in the ground while Peter and Rebecca cleared away a few stray leaves and branches. Peter said he would put a bench down there for us to rest on when we were tired of gardening and just needed to stop for a while. Rebecca retired to bed right afterward. She seemed weak, pale and red-eyed, but had been unable to rest until the baby was interred. She told me later that night that she thought it might have been a boy, and she sobbed silently into my shoulder, saying how she disappointed Peter. I tried to comfort her and she finally fell into a fitful sleep.

Chapter 39 – Sarah

That afternoon, after we had worked until we were exhausted, Harry excused himself, saying he had to get back to the office. The rest of us went out again for pizza, which I was quite tired of by this point. Alice and Bea went home from there, and Betsy and Maureen and I went back to the house. I pulled out a nice Cabernet and we sat down to chew the fat. I knew they were close to bursting with questions. They just loved Alice and could see that Harry was not exactly run of the mill, but a pretty nice fellow. And, of course, they thought Bea was a hot sketch. So, how was I handling all this? Obviously I had two charming suitors. They started asking all the predictable questions.

"Well, sorry gals, I just don't know if I'm gay, but if I were, Alice would be an attractive candidate. And Harry? I don't know, he is truly nice, appealing, and successful, but, I just don't think I'm ready for any of it right now. I'm at the point in my life where I don't want, or need to fool around anymore. I don't want to date. I'm not even sure I want to test the waters. It may change, but that's just where I am right now. I just want to get myself together and settled in. Then, I'll see. But I don't think I want to rush into something serious yet."

As much as they understood my position, they thought that each was a catch, and I shouldn't let both of them get away. People like that don't come along every day and could be snapped up any moment.

"Well," I said, "It's just going to be a chance I'll have to take." They finally let it go, and we talked into the wee hours about the journals, which I was revealing to them in enticing pieces. With each new revelation, they squealed with excitement. I had to finish the latest entries before I could reveal them to anyone as this was the most delicate of subjects. My grandmother had sex with her husband. Oh, the shame of it all! When viewed from another perspective, it all seemed so odd.

I was lucky enough to still have a single mattress in the small spare bedroom, so while Betsy and Maureen stayed in my new room I had a reasonably comfortable place to sleep. I could easily spend one night there. My friends had worked so hard for me and I was happy knowing they would be comfortable and, after all, they were going to leave the next day. I felt so fortunate to have such good friends and family.

We went out to breakfast the next day and I drove them into the town center, past the garage where Alice worked, past the little mill where Doris had worked for a while after moving to the country. I explained to Betsy and Maureen some of the history of the local textile industry and the mill girls who worked there.

I was fascinated with the mill girls and the lives they must have led. And as we drove by these old mills and I talked of what their lives were like, Betsy and Maureen listened thoughtfully. This was a whole way of life with which most people were unfamiliar.

"Geeze, Sarah, this, it's fascinating. And to think this is how your grandmother lived and where she worked."

"Yeah, it gives me a strangely comforting feeing of wholeness, of connection to the past, my past, and theirs. It's almost as though I was meant to find the journals, like they left them for me. They could never have shared a whole lifetime with me, all the difficulties and joys." I pointed out the building where the mill library was housed and then the old Elms boarding house as we drove by. It took us about 20 minutes to drive into town from the old homestead, but Bea said when she used to train into Willimantic it took almost 30 minutes, it was a pretty ride following the river.

Chapter 40 – Doris

Sun. Apr. 23, 1899

The world seems to have become more and more strange. Rebecca's depression after losing the baby was heart wrenching. She was inconsolable at first. We all grieved, but Becky was so sad that her health began to fail. I could do nothing to help her. I did the cooking and fed her, but she stayed in bed much of the day. I felt I had to go to work but would come home for lunch as often as I dared, to give her broth and tea. Then, an idea came to me. It was a fine spring day and Peter was out working in the garden. He had a passion for the garden and as soon as the soil began to dry he was busy there. I know he too felt helpless with Rebecca's illness. We sat out on the front porch. She had a lap blanket on and a cup of tea that I had brought her. We both sat there watching Peter dig and get down on his knees and work the soil with a trowel, putting in little seeds and pulling out emerging weeds.

"I will have the baby" I said. I didn't know where it came from, or whose voice it was. Rebecca looked at me. "I will have the baby." I repeated, more definitely, nodding my head. She continued to stare at me. I got up, went over, hugged and kissed her and said, "It will be all right, we will be a happy family again." I saw her sit up straighter and her eyes followed me, questioning my statement. But her face lightened and she looked as though the heaviest weight she could ever carry had been lifted from her. It was that obvious, as though she had been laboring under a heavy weight and once that weight was lifted, she smiled.

"Really? You would do that? You could do that?"

"Yes, darling, for you I would do anything," and it was true. "But you will have to help me, as I am afraid." She nodded.

"Yes, I can help."

Both of us looked over at Peter, the sun on his back, his straw hat almost falling off as he wiped the sweat away from his face, then we looked back at each other and smiled.

And that is how it came about. That evening, at supper after we told Peter what we were thinking, he looked from one to the other and back.

Finally, I broke the silence. "Well, what do you think?" but Peter was still distilling this news.

"Well, I guess that would work, but are you sure you both agree to this?" He looked again from one to the other, trying to see any hidden emotions. But he only saw smiling faces, and this was a great relief to him.

We had thought to do it as soon as possible, but I was fearful and needed fortifying. We agreed upon the next weekend and also agreed not to tell William just yet.

Sun. Apr. 30, 1899

Well, it is done. It was not as hard as my wild imagination had anticipated. I know this will sound very queer, but Rebecca was there with me, in the dark, she lay next to me, kissing me and encouraging me. I know that Peter was awkward and hesitant to have us both there, and that must have been difficult, but we carried it off. I refused to remove all my clothes so that we were all in the bed, clothed. I'm sure it was a sight that would have turned the local pastor's hair white. It was painful at first. I'm not sure why women would consent to do this except to conceive, but it is over. And now we all wait to see if a baby will come of it.

Sun. May 14, 1899

No news of a baby yet, either way. I am still working, but we discussed this and have made plans. If we find that a baby is coming, I will work for another month and then ask for my papers and leave with a recommendation. Then I will stay home, actually, both Rebecca and I will stay home, because the village would be all in a dither if I became pregnant. We will both need to remain in seclusion for the whole time. We can have the baby in Rebecca's room and in case we need a doctor we would get one from out of town who doesn't know us.

Sun. Jun 4, 1899

I think I am going to have a baby. I am quitting my job this Friday. I am giving the excuse that Rebecca is pregnant and I must tend to her, as I am the housekeeper. We are all getting hopeful that this will be successful and that there will be no problems. We've told William, whose eyes filled with tears. He is such a dear, tender fellow. I am feeling fine so far, actually feeling very healthy and fit and full of life. I'm excited and frightened by the prospect of this new adventure.

Sun. Jul. 16, 1899

The baby grows within me now, and I feel healthy, happy, and good. I am helping in the garden and around the house. William is thrilled and sends over the finest little treats for me as my appetite grows steadily. I feel like a queen bee with all my dears hovering around looking for little pleasures to give me.

Sun. Aug. 20, 1899

I continue to be healthy and am still easily able to do things around the house and yard. How happy I feel, filled with a wonderful feeling of contentment and satisfaction and wellbeing which seem to follow me all day long. Everyone notes it and encourages me.

Sun. Sept. 17, 1899

I have become noticeably larger, but most of my clothes still fit. When no one watches, Rebecca lays her head upon my stomach and talks to the baby, promising to read to her and love her and makes up silly nonsense rhymes for her. Rebecca thinks it will be a girl, but I think it will be a boy. Peter says that he only wants it to be healthy, and we all plan for our little baby. We are starting to harvest our first crops, so we are canning and pickling and putting up lots of our vegetables.

Sat. Oct. 21, 1899

My clothes are becoming very tight, I can no longer cinch the waist on my dresses and I'm grateful for clothes that fit. Rebecca is reading a book on childbirth, as she hopes to be the midwife and wants to be prepared. Peter has been working in his shop behind the house making a little cradle.

Sat. Nov. 18, 1899

All progresses well and everyone gathers when the baby is restless to feel the kicks and movements it makes, holding their hands to my stomach. Even Peter is talking to the little one now, putting his head against my stomach and humming little songs. The baby grows larger daily. I don't seem to be able to eat enough, I want to eat everything, and I have odd cravings for food which everyone tries to satisfy. Bananas and the beautiful black olives which William sometimes brings me are my favorites.

Sun Dec. 17, 1899

It has become difficult to stand up from a seated position, and I find I must go to the toilet often. The kicks are more pronounced and the baby more active. I am glad it is during the winter as even in the cold, I feel hot. My feet and my back hurt, and I find it hard to roll over in bed and find a comfortable position to sleep.

Tues. Jan. 30, 1900

I went into seclusion yesterday; I am very uncomfortable now and will be happy to be done with this. I feel the time must be close and that the baby is determined to be born soon. This has been an amazing experience and I am happy to have been able to do this for Peter and Rebecca and myself, but I hope this will come to a happy end soon.

Wed. Jan. 31, 1900

We have a girl, a beautiful little baby girl! Rebecca was a perfect midwife, and our little baby was born without any difficulties, but with more pain than I could ever have imagined. The birth was not complicated which was fortunate because the raging snow storm would have made it very difficult for Peter to go get a doctor. Although we will be raising her under the pretense that she is Rebecca's, they let me name her, and I have decided upon Beatrice, which is my Mother's name. She is a miracle. She sleeps on my breast now. We all sleep together, me, Beatrice and Rebecca. Peter knocks and peeks in and smiles and comes over and pets her and kisses us both on the cheek. What a strange and wonderful family I now have.

William talks of nothing but how he will take her out on the pony as soon as she is able. He brings little toys that she is not yet able to use, but which are so cute. He is such a fawning uncle.

I nurse her, cradle and rock her and then Rebecca does too. Rebecca is so charmed by her little fingers and toes, she bathes her and changes and washes her clothes. I am still not allowed to do any work. Everyone waits upon me as though I were unable to take care of myself. I'm sure I will tire of this soon.

Chapter 41 – Sarah

I've started my new job and fallen into the rhythm of it with ease, being able to bring the skills and good practices with me to enhance their processes. I'm making friends and fitting right in, it's hard to believe I've only been there a month I feel so comfortable. I hope that the good experience I'm having will last for a long time and not just be the first blush of excitement over the new job.

Alice came over frequently the first week I moved in, helping me to paint and clean, move furniture and carry boxes. After that I hardly saw her. It was strange, as though she'd just dropped out of sight. I called her a couple of times but got no answer.

Harry came over occasionally, but he was busy with his work. He would pop in unexpectedly since he was so close and when he had an hour or two he'd stop by with a grinder or a dozen eggs. He came by one day and fixed the railing on the porch. Another time, on the way to a quick lunch together, we stopped by his office to check up on one of the animals. A dog who had been hit by a car and Harry had operated on hours earlier. The family who owned him was worried, but Harry had stitched him up and set the broken leg and now had him sedated. Harry was gentle and soothing in his tone with the dog, which tried to get up, but Harry petted him and the dog lay back down letting out a big sigh. There was going to be a happy ending to that story. There were moments when I felt I could really like this guy, so simple and straight-forward and with a disarming smile and gentle demeanor.

When Bea met me for dinner and said that Alice stopped by and had her ex-girlfriend Joyce with her, I became concerned. I knew Joyce was alluring, attractive and cruel. She didn't like that Alice had chosen to work at the garage. Joyce wanted Alice to be a white collar worker, a professional. But Alice disappointed her in that area, so Joyce would drop sarcastic remarks about Alice's choice of professions and aim to humiliate her whenever she got the opportunity. Eventually Joyce got together with a lawyer, but that soured and now she must have come back to Alice, who once had strong feelings for her. I wasn't sure how I felt about Alice, but I knew I liked her as a friend and I didn't like to think that she was being preyed upon by a gold digger who cared more about her lover's career than about her actual wellbeing.

The pit in my stomach grew to the point that my appetite for the pizza in front of me disappeared. I had been growing tired of pizza anyway and now it almost turned my stomach. I was sad that Alice couldn't make the break that she needed to and would consider reuniting with someone who was clearly abusive and cheated on her, but I couldn't be certain that I was the one to fill the void for her.

"I see." It was all I could say. I didn't know how to handle this or even if I should try. Alice was an adult. She could make her own decisions about whom she should or shouldn't be dating. I didn't like feeling as though my life was bordering on the edge of drama. All I wanted was to settle down into a nice, quiet life.

When I got home I opened a bottle of wine, and settled in to read the paper, and then the diaries – I needed a diversion. How could I have known that the drama was not over?

Chapter 42 – Doris

Sat. Feb. 10, 1900

Our little Bea is a dear baby, she barely ever cries and when she does, half a dozen arms reach out to hold her. She eats well and has already grown. We are all in love with her. Although she doesn't yet sleep through the night, when she wakes, I nurse her and then Rebecca settles her in to sleep, hoping that it will last until dawn so that we may sleep also.

Sun. Apr. 15, 1900

Bea is sleeping longer in the night and grows fast. We think she is a smart and perfect baby. William came and brought with him a lovely baby carriage for her. Rebecca and I walk her up and down the street, over to William's and back, so she will get some fresh air.

Sun. Jul. 8, 1900

We are putting Bea into a cradle at night now and she almost sleeps all through the night. We walk her often and take her out under the shade of the trees and we all watch Peter work in the garden and mow the small lawn.

Sat. Oct. 13, 1900

As our little family becomes comfortable and Rebecca and I can get sleep in our bed together again, another unusual request came to me by way of William. I cannot say that this was totally unexpected, as on occasion, he has hinted at his proposal, but I was able to pretend I didn't understand. As you can guess, William wants an heir. He wants a son, someone to help with the farm and give him grandchildren. At first I was angry with him, he having approached the subject when only we two were together. I told him I was not a vessel for child bearing and other responses that I could see surprised and saddened him. Then, after having given it more thought, and realizing how kind he was, not just kind, but that he obviously would be a fine parent, I told him I would do this. But the proposition would be under the same terms as those with Peter. Rebecca would help see me through the initial conception. I would, with everyone's help, of course, raise the child until it could be fed by itself and then turn it over to William and his housekeeper. If it turned out to be a girl, I did not want to try a second time. He would have to accept that a girl would be his heir. William agreed to this and the plan was undertaken. I cannot believe I am to say this, but Peter was also in attendance at this conception. We all had a light dinner and several glasses of wine and we tried to make light of it. Peter helped William and Rebecca caressed me. We were nearly fully clothed and Peter pulled a quilt over us in the dark. It was all a tangle of arms and legs and I had Rebecca's caresses to help me. I think we were all in muss.

William wasn't sure how he would explain the child if I conceived, but maybe, he thought to say he was adopting a cousin's baby after the wife died. So, now, we find, I am again having a child, I expect by next June. We will be a larger, happier family.

Tues, Jan. 8, 1901

Beatrice has taken her first steps. Holding onto Rebecca's apron, she stands and then strikes out. She is such a chubby, busy baby. I am growing larger and this time I don't feel I need to stay secluded. If neighbors find me pregnant, I don't care. I will let them believe that William is the father, as he is, but that I cannot marry, but must care for Rebecca and Peter and Bea. But we rarely socialize so I don't think this will become a topic of much gossip. We have, all four, thought about William and I getting married, just to make it easier. I would continue to stay here, but we have yet to fully agree on it.

Fri., Mar. 15, 1901

Again, I am getting larger and find it a little harder to help in the garden and around the house, but instead try to watch Bea who is moving about with liveliness now. She calls me Auntie Doris and calls Rebecca Mama. Rebecca is so thrilled with this it makes me happy to see how much she enjoys being a mother.

Mon, Jun. 10, 1901

Rebecca, my dear Rebecca, has saved our son.

It is a boy, a beautiful boy, but he came early and the cord was about his neck and Rebecca pulled it off and puffed the life into him.

William was waiting outside our door and nearly burst with joy when Rebecca let him in to see the little one. William is going to name him Michael. We all held him and little Bea touched him. We are the perfect family now. I am exhausted and Rebecca, having had quite a fright, seems equally exhausted. We three lay in the bed with the boys, William and Peter bringing us tea and biscuits and little Bea yelping to be put up on the bed.

Mon. Jul. 15, 1901

Little Michael fusses more than Bea did, he cries a little more and eats more too. But he is our little man. Where does the time go?

Sun. Sep. 22, 1901

William has taken his son Michael out for a walk in the baby carriage. Peter walks with them, Bea holding his hand, all walking together. Rebecca and I take this time to have the intimacy that we so rarely get these days; we hope to have more as Bea grows up. My dear Rebecca, she has my heart, and has seen me through so much, how dearly I love her.

Sun. July 12, 1908

What an odd day we had, I must add this to my little book. Rebecca and I were shopping today at the five and ten, when we ran into Esther! Esther of all people. Esther, and her husband, a little milk toast looking man. We were cordial and pointed at Bea in the toy aisle and told her that was our daughter. She looked dumbfounded; it was such a satisfying stroke. We left the store, hand in hand with Bea between us. We went to meet Peter at the railroad station. Bea begged us to walk across the footbridge and back, watching the trains below and waving at the engineers. It was an endless fascination for her. We met Peter as he came out of the barbershop down on Railroad Street and Bea called to him from the footbridge above and waved. And we told him of our encounter with Esther. We all had a good laugh as we ate our French peanuts on the train ride home.

I cannot believe how quickly time goes by. We have been so busy with Bea that I have not had a moment to write, and I miss it. She is getting big and I am proud to say she's quite smart and lively. Our good fortune is without measure.

Chapter 43 – Sarah

The next morning I called Alice at the garage. I had to tell someone and I was hoping she would want to hear the latest saga from the journal.

"Oh! You won't believe what I've just read. Can you meet me at the diner for lunch?"

"Yeah, I guess so." She sounded hesitant.

"I just have to talk to you."

As we ate lunch, I described Peter and Rebecca trying to conceive and Rebecca losing the baby, and Doris trying to conceive and having the baby, having Bea.

"I'll tell you, if I didn't read it, I wouldn't believe it. But when I think about it now, it makes sense. I mean Bea and I are built much more like Doris than like Rebecca, who was a smaller woman even before she'd shrunk. Bea had lighter hair. Rebecca's was darker in the pictures. So it's probably all true." Alice was well into her BLT but I had hardly touched my Rueben because I couldn't stop talking. "I don't know what to do. I don't think I should tell Bea. How do you tell someone that, for her whole life, the woman who she thought was her Mother was not? How do you reconcile that, especially now that both of them are dead?"

"I can't believe it. That's amazing." Alice was as flabbergasted as I was.

"I was thrown for a loop. I don't know what else happens because I haven't finished it, but geeze, it is just unbelievable, that old adage about fact being stranger than fiction…" I paused long enough to get a couple bites of the Rueben and a sip of soda. "Ok, if you think that's incredible, wait until you hear this. After having Peter's baby, William approaches Bea and asks her to have his baby, and even though she's feeling rather put upon, I mean this isn't like asking if you could pick me up something from the store, she agrees. And…" I paused for another bite and sip of soda.

"This is the limit, she has the baby, it's a boy. Do you know what his name is?" I pause for effect, "Michael." "MICHAEL!" I said with more emphasis.

"Michael?" Alice sounded confused. "Michael?" She repeated, as though she wasn't making the connection. Then after a long pause, "Let me see if I get this straight, you mean that Aunt Doris is your real grandmother?"

"Yes." I nod my head, smiling, thinking, yes, she gets it.

"And she's Harry's real grandmother too?"

"Yes! Unbelievable, huh?

"Holy shit." Alice lets out a big sigh. "I didn't think I had a snowball's chance in Hell with you, with, you know, with Harry hanging around and all. Then Joyce came back and, well…"

I could do nothing but laugh out loud.

Chapter 44 – Doris

Fri. May 11, 1917

We are so upset. Our little Bea has hurt us more that I can describe. She's growing up, growing tall and becoming a woman, but inside she's still a child. She wants to be independent, we worry that we haven't given her enough, haven't been the best parents we could have been to her. She hides in her room and reads, or goes out for long walks, or goes to friends houses. She seems to avoid us. When she's not able to avoid us, she's angry with us, and sometimes says cruel things to us. It's hurt us, but Peter seems most affected of all. He says it may have been wrong for us to try and raise a child in a home like this, that maybe we should have not tried to raise a family, but just stayed alone in the house. Now that we have her though, and she is so smart and pretty, I don't know if I would think of giving up what we've had with her, even if she doesn't speak to us ever again. We have brought this amazing person into the world and she has thrived. I hope that she will outgrow this, but it is difficult waiting for this season of discontent to pass. Will she hate us once she realizes our secrets or will she someday forgive us? No matter what, we will love her.

September, 1929

Dear book, how strange to write that again, it has been years since I entered a word into this book. So many years have passed, and so much has happened. I had almost forgotten about this book, I had tucked it so far back into the drawer, and only found it when I was cleaning. Life became too busy to write, too busy to do anything but live it.

As I read back through this I see our strange and wonderful lives take shape and the twists and turns that directed them to where we are today.

Bea is now grown, graduated from college. College! We scraped to send her and she was able work and save a lot herself. She's done so well for herself. We had some hard times, money was tight and we were lucky to have William to help us with a good pot roast or ham now and then, without that, we'd have had beans and potatoes almost every night. Sometimes Rebecca would find Bea tossing out a worn down bar of soap and just about hit the roof. Poor Bea. She finally ran off with that fellow she'd been dating. They got married. Rebecca was relieved at that, but none of us like the boy very much. Well, we told her, she can always come back if married life doesn't suit her.

Peter's health is failing, but Rebecca and I care for him as we would a child. He becomes cranky, but we know that it is mostly that he misses William. Dear William is gone. He died last year when a tree he was felling crushed him. Peter misses him very much, he says little, but mopes about and often walks slowly down to the farm and back. I think the only solace he has is gardening, when it seems he is at peace and we all make much of his lovely gardens and often go out and sit with him there.

Michael is grown and has done a good job taking over the farm. He married and already they have a baby boy, Harry. William did not get to see that little baby, but knew that it was due, and just knowing that made him happy. We like to imagine he died fulfilled.

Michael has grown away from us though, and we are all sad for that. He doesn't come to visit us here and doesn't invite us over there. I miss him, our little man; he spent so much time with us when he was young, he was like Bea's brother, and now we hardly see him at all. Bea comes home to us often during work vacations, so we have the comfort of her smiling face, joking with Peter and going for walks with us and helping us around the house.

I am happy. I have had a rich and full life and I wouldn't change a bit of it, and not many people can say that.

Ah, here comes Rebecca, to take my hand and draw me out for a walk along the lane. My dearest Rebecca.

Chapter 45 – Sarah

Bea came over to my new house for a celebratory dinner. It's barely been a month since I've moved in and several since we buried Rebecca. I made a spaghetti dinner and got a good Chianti and we sat down to spend a nice evening with just the two of us. It's been hard getting some time together, with me renovating and working, and people visiting frequently. Having a few hours to spend alone together seems like a rare treat. Knowing what the journals held made me more curious about Bea and her perspective on her childhood and parents but I wasn't sure how to approach the subject, or just how much I thought she would want to know.

"So what's happening with you?" I started after serving up the spaghetti and pouring us both a healthy glass of Chianti.

"Oh, nothing much. I'm putting in a little time down at the lawyers, giving them some help with their books. Boy, that was a mess, and we've pretty much got it straightened out. It always surprises me how some problems are just ignored, swept under the carpet as though they didn't exist."

"Really?" I was thinking this might be my opening to divert the conversation. "Do you think people just pretend not to see what they don't want to deal with? Don't you find people funny, how people go about avoiding those things that seem difficult?"

"I see where you're going with this; don't try to be foxy about it. This is about Cheryl, isn't it? I knew you'd get around to asking since I never told you what happened." Bea put her fork down, took a sip of the Chianti and put both hands on the table next to her plate. I could see this was a sensitive subject, but I waited to see what she would do. "All right, you probably should know. It's a bizarre story, okay, but remember this happened a few years ago." Bea took a deep breath and another sip of the wine. "You know how close Cheryl and I were, we were just the best of friends. We did everything together, raised you kids together, shopped, sometimes vacationed when Mitch, you remember Mitch, who never seemed to be home? Well sometimes when she didn't vacation with Mitch we'd all go to the shore and rent a cottage – remember those times at Misquamicut? Those were good times. Anyway, one evening, we were all having dinner together and Mitch was home. You were upstairs sleeping with the other kids. We were downstairs and well into our second bottle of wine, when Cheryl went to the kitchen to set up some cheese and crackers. Mitch, who was sitting next to me on the couch, leaned over and laid a big kiss on me, grabbing my tit and mumbling something about how crazy he was about me. I was flabbergasted. I got up so fast and rushed into the kitchen. I must have looked flushed and nervous. I went over to the kitchen sink and splashed some cold water onto my face and lips. I felt so violated. I wanted to tell Cheryl, but I couldn't, not then. I started to avoid Mitch when he was around. Then it happened again, when we were all there together for dinner, and I was still trying to avoid him but he was clever and while I was washing dishes he came in and told Cheryl that he thought he heard one of the kids cry out. Well, she rushed upstairs and he came up behind me at the sink, grabbed my tits, pushed up against me and kissed the back of my neck. That was it. I dropped the plate in the sink, rushed out and just couldn't go back. Cheryl never knew; I never told her. She asked, and we would still do things together, but the friendship just cooled. You were getting older, I was even afraid for you. That was when I told you to go straight home when you got out of school, and that I would leave a snack for you; I didn't want you going over there. We just drifted apart, Cheryl and me. it was sad. She was my best friend, like a sister, but her damned husband was a creep. I don't know how many other women he messed around with, but it killed our friendship." Bea looked into her wine glass, swirling it around, looking thoughtful. She took a sip and toyed with the spaghetti, and then she went on.

"You know, Rebecca and Aunt Doris; that was real love, there was no cheating there, no loss of devotion. I saw it most profoundly in the last few weeks and days as Doris was languishing, and when she died, I'll never forget it. Years after Pete died, when Doris was sick, Rebecca tended her gently every day, reading to her, feeding her, bathing her. I would stop by now and then and it was clear that Doris was fading rapidly. I was there that day, the day she died; she didn't even seem to know we were there. Rebecca was holding her hand, leaning close to her face talking gently to her as Doris was taking those last breaths. Then Doris exhaled and her body relaxed. Rebecca, felt it, felt her soul leave. She was still holding her hand and she started to sob, then wail, this long loud inhuman wail. On and on she went like this. I was embarrassed to be there, to be witnessing this most profound expression of grief. She keened on and on. Then, out of the blue, like some kind of vision, another scene flashed before my eyes.

I remembered one day when I went out for a walk, I came upon a little bird dead on the side of the road. It seemed to be just killed by a car, it was still warm. I moved it off the road and gently laid it in the grass, and all the while, as it lay there, its mate sat in the tree above it singing, singing, fluttering closer and singing. Trying to sing it alive, trying to wake it up, trying to get her to rise up and fly away with him. Rebecca was that bird, wailing to wake her, wailing to bring her back for a last breath, a last second. But she knew that her wailing wouldn't wake Doris, she knew that her life's partner was gone forever." Bea was looking down at her wine, and took another sip.

"I knew before then, I guess I always knew. I didn't resent either of them. All I could see at that moment was someone who loved another person so much that her life was torn asunder. Doris was a part of Rebecca and Rebecca was a part of Doris and losing one was going to kill the other."

"How can you fault someone for loving too much? Is there a sin in that, or is the sin in not loving at all?"

Bea looked at me, long and intense. "All I can say is, be sure of whom you want to spend your life with, be sure of whom you love. Don't be swayed by convention, it's best to follow your heart, without fear, no matter where it leads you." With that, Bea signaled she was done talking. "Hey this stuff is cold, want to go down to Angelo's and get some hot spaghetti?" She started to get up, waiting for me to see if I would follow.

"You bet, let me get my wallet. This time it really is my treat."

As we headed out the door, I continued, "I remember when you told me to go straight home after school. It seemed strange to me at the time and it made me sad. I really liked visiting Cheryl and the kids and I missed that as part of my daily routine. They were sort of my family, I missed them. Wow, so that's what happened? It's not what I expected. Somewhere, I was imagining something happening, you know, between you and Cheryl, that's why I didn't bring it up again. I thought you didn't want to talk to me about something like that."

Bea almost choked, and let out a big howl, "Holy Cows, no wonder you weren't more inquisitive. Well, there never was anything like that between us. Like I said, we were close, she was like the sister I never had, and I still miss her, but I couldn't abide by that sleazy husband of hers."

"Tell me more. Do you know where she went? Are you sure she didn't know? Why did they move?" I was bursting with questions about Cheryl, but any questions I had, about whom was right for me had been answered.

Chapter 46 – Sarah

I had to tell Harry about Rebecca and Doris, William and Peter. I wasn't sure if Bea could take it, but I thought it would only be fair to Harry to share it with him.

So, a couple days after reading the latest chapter, I asked him to come over to dinner, pot roast I told him. He sounded very pleased and said he'd bring the wine.

The house was looking pretty good these days and the yard too. Work still needed to be done, but it felt and looked like a home. So when he drove up with a little shrub and a big bottle of wine, I imagined he intended a house warming celebration. He even asked me to get the shovel out and we picked out a place in the yard for the azalea and he planted it.

I dished out the pot roast and buttered some warm biscuits while he poured the wine and set the table.

We settled in for a nice meal, he toasted me and the house, and leaned across the table and touched my hand. I may have looked a little oddly at him, but to recover, I took the journals from the counter and put them on the table.

"I have something very personal to share with you, something that touches us both." He looked at me intently, sipping his wine. "These," I put my hand on them, "Are Rebecca's and Aunt Doris's journals." Harry nodded and smiled. "They are very personal, and I've been reading them for the last several months." He smiled and nodded expectantly. "They are about how they met and how they became friends and how their lives also intertwined with other lives, like Peter's." He nodded, his brow furrowed, beginning to realize there was a reason I was going so tediously slow.

"Ok, so what's in them? Is it a big drama?"

"Well, actually, yes it is. It isn't just about Peter; it's about William and Peter."

"Yeah, OK, they were neighbors for decades. William helped them get settled here, sold them the land."

"Right," I said, getting ready to dig in to the hard part. "Well, things weren't as they appeared."

Harry's eyebrows went up, "OK?"

"I'm going to try and start at the beginning, so be patient and listen." I started to tell him about Rebecca and Doris meeting and that they were very close. He grimaced. "Be patient," I said gently. "Well, they were discovered in bed and in a desperate attempt to stay together, Rebecca married Peter, but the women stayed together. William helped Peter, Rebecca and Doris set up here in this house and held the mortgage until they paid it off. He also helped with lots of other things around here."

"OK? This much I know. I guess I'm surprised. I mean that is an uncommon arrangement, your grandmother and Aunt Doris and Peter? Wow."

"Well, there's more to the story. So, have a sip and I'll tell you the rest." He took a sip and I took a bite of what was becoming cold pot roast.

"So, after they moved in, Rebecca revealed to Doris that the agreement was that she would have Peter's child. It was the only way, she explained, that the situation would look fairly normal. So they tried to conceive, but Becky wasn't fertile or healthy enough to carry full term. So, Doris, to help Rebecca, agreed to have the baby, little Beatrice."

"Oh. Huh? So Rebecca isn't your grandmother, Doris is?"

"Exactly, but here is where it gets more complicated. William wanted a child too. He wasn't married, not planning to get married, and Doris conceived and had his baby, little Michael." This is when Harry choked on the sip of wine.

"What? Come on. I don't believe it. This is a joke." He snorted. "It's very creative, but if you want to tell me you don't want to date, you don't have to go to this length."

"It's not a joke. These are old journals, why would anyone make up such an elaborate story and put it in a journal?"

"I don't believe it. It just is so fantastic; that we could have the same grandmother."

"Yes, and I'm thinking, although it's not written in the journals, that Peter and Michael may have been very, you know, close."

"Oh, my God. You know what? That's probably why Dad has always been so weird about Peter, and the gals here. He never said anything, but it seemed like there was something going on that I never understood. I wonder what he knows. I wonder if he would ever talk to me about it."

"So, what does that make us anyway? First cousins? Step siblings?"

"Kissing cousins?" Harry laughed as he reached across the table and held my hand. With his other hand he lifted his glass, "To small towns and close neighbors."

I smiled, withdrew my hand, clinked glasses with him, "Hear, hear," was all I said, but my thoughts went to Alice.

Chapter 47 – Sarah

I wouldn't say it was an accident. I think both of us knew it was going to happen. So one Friday evening, after a couple of beers when I asked Alice to my house, she gave me a piercing look, cocked her head and raised her eye brows. I smiled, nodded slightly and we both reached for our keys. Since then, she has rarely gone back to her apartment.

We have fallen into a comfortable pattern of working and coming to my house to make dinner, and sometimes reading or going for a walk, or going to bed early. Finally, what seemed like my standard dinners of pizza and grinders has turned into more healthy and varied fare, as we both enjoy cooking and especially cooking together.

"So, what's on the menu tonight?" I ask with curiosity.

"I was thinking about romaine lettuce salad with a little grilled chicken?" Alice had gone shopping as she often did when she got out of work before me.

"Mmmm, sounds good, want some help?"

"Sure, if you wash and prep the lettuce and other salad fixings, I'll grill the chicken. What do you say?"

"Okay," I said as I went to the sink with the greens, ready to wash them. We had a relaxed meal. Alice talked about the town news she heard which she liked to share with me. It seemed like the garage was one of the places where people gathered to pass time talking about their neighbors and the latest happenings. Alice always got an earful and so kept me up to date with the goings on. I tried not to talk too much about work, especially if it involved someone she might know, she understood this discretion. Then talk usually turned to what went on during our day.

"So, you know I've been transcribing those journals, remember all the improbable twists and turns? I've been thinking about it. How did they all find each other? How odd is it that they all found each other and were able to have such a good outcome from what seemed destined to be a sad future?"

Alice paused to digest this. "I don't know. How did we meet each other, how odd was that? You had that flat tire and I happened to be the person to come along and fix it. That Harry would be a relative and not just the handsome vet next door. There are so many improbable and impossible outcomes, and we make the best of them. We bend a little to fit, we change a little, we try to work it all out to the best possible conclusion. We certainly are not rigid."

"I can't wait for you to read them. They are just full of love and sacrifice and longing; real-life drama. Do you think people will look back on our lives and think we had full, beautiful and loving lives, filled with drama and excitement? Or will they seem dull, mundane and common? I can't say this is the life I expected to end up with, or the one I had planned. Life is strange and wonderful." Alice could only nod her head in agreement.

"So, why did you choose me? I mean you had the handsome vet next door who seemed very interested, was it because he was a relative? Did that really matter?" Alice mused as she dried the dishes.

"It wasn't a choice. It was what I was feeling, but I think mostly on a subconscious level. I remember that first time we met, when you jumped out of the truck smiling and making easy small talk, I felt something even then, an excitement, a thrill, but I was in total denial of my feelings and attributed them to other things. I was telling myself I needed a new friend, a good friend, a confidant, I hadn't had someone like that in years. It was providence that we clicked right away. But I found it hard to accept my feelings, hard to go against convention. It frightened me and I denied my real feelings. My grandmother was an inspiration. She left everything to follow her lover, not knowing where it would lead her or how it would turn out. She just got on that train to an unknown future with just her bandbox and the faith that her love would be there and carry her through. And then Bea gave me the talk, you know, the look-into-your-heart talk, and basically gave me permission to follow my heart wherever it might lead me. So here I am, glad to be starting a new life in my hometown, in my grandparent's home, with a fine lady mechanic." Alice saw me pick up my nearly empty wine glass from the side of the sink, and reached for hers.

"To an interesting and lively future." We clinked the glasses and drained the last drops.

"So," I started in on a sensitive subject "It's been a couple of months and you've been just about living here; isn't it time that you moved in? Is there something I don't know that's holding you back?" I knew she was concerned about the future, afraid that once we truly were living together things would change. If she still had her rooms, she could always get away if she needed to, moving in seemed so final, and it would probably get all over town.

"You could have your own room." I bargained, "You could have Doris's room." She turned and looked hard at me.

"I know you mean well, and I know it's a sensible request, but…" Alice paused and took my hand, "I'm just not ready yet."

"I guess I understand, but it hurts a little, I'll leave the room open for a while, but someday I may stop asking."

"I understand. Come on now; let's go out for an evening walk." She pulled me towards the door, giving me just enough time to grab a sweater before we headed out the door.

Chapter 48 – Doris

May, 1934

Hi book, I am back. It again seems like an eternity since I have last written in this book. It seems like only for the big events now.

Peter is gone, he became so weak and distraught since he could no longer help us around the house and felt useless. He didn't want to go to the hospital and made us swear we would never take him. We watched him slide downhill, stop eating, then stop drinking, and finally just slip away. We will miss him. He was so strong and solid, and dependable, so steady in his ways.

We buried him next to William. Michael protested, but we had purchased the lot next to William's so we could do this without creating a stir, we just buried them next to each other with different head stones. It is too bad that Michael is so difficult about his father.

But, dear book, here is the best news. We have a granddaughter. She is a beauty, smart as a whip and just as independent as Bea, but not quite as precocious. Little Sarah, her hair is blonde, with a touch of red, and she is tall and thin. Peter loved to watch her in the garden eating the tomatoes, and smelling the flowers and watching the insects, just like Bea had. He loved Bea's wild streak, but Sarah is more serious. We are so fortunate. Bea has done well for herself, but does not seem to be able to have a good marriage. Did we fail somewhere? Still, she brings Sarah over often. We are rich beyond measure. Ah, the robin's evening song, it's time to go.

Chapter 49 – Sarah

When Bea called and said she would come over today and that she wanted to take me, Alice and Harry out for a drive, I dressed warmly as she had hinted it would be an outside jaunt.

She drove through the town and then on the outskirts, pulled into the cemetery. In the newer section, where Rebecca was buried, she stopped in front of a highly polished headstone, got out and motioned for the rest of us to follow.

We walked over to a modest stone and Bea pointed at it.

Rebecca Moorhouse
And
Doris Biracree
They walked the road together
Hand in hand, a bond
Forged by the fires of
Enduring devotion and
Everlasting love

We all stared in silence, each of us in our own thoughts, each of us with our own conceptions about them. A powerful feeling overtook me. I felt a warm, engulfing embrace, at the moment. I imagined I felt my grandmothers embracing me. It gave me a sense of deep contentment and a feeling of wholeness or full circle that I cannot explain. Had they fulfilled a quest that none of us knew about, or understood, not even they, themselves?

No one had the intimate knowledge of them that I did, and at that moment, I decided no one else would.

Chapter 50 – Sarah

I'd been getting comfortable at my new job, gaining experience and an understanding of their business practices. Generally, I liked everyone and they were happy with me and my work. I even made a few good friends there who would meet me after work for a drink or dinner.

Alice finally relented and moved in, she realized most people in town already knew we were "an item" as she put it, and it didn't seem to change how she was viewed. She said what changed her mind was watching me in the garden. Down on my knees, dirty, sweaty, bugs swarming about and pulling out weeds, talking to the plants, intent on giving each one the attention it required. It's what got her, that focus, that caring. She realized that I was the person who fit with her best. That puzzle piece of the psyche, the mechanic and the gardener. How could I be anything but sincere and caring? She was able to trust a relationship again. Enough to move the few things she had left at her little apartment into the other bedroom and finally hand the keys in.

Even before she formally moved in, we had gradually been upgrading the old house, fixing what we could and calling in contractors when we had the cash to pay them and putting emergency repairs on credit when we didn't. The old furnace finally had to be replaced and it was a spectacularly gross expense. So I was grateful for our vegetable garden which gave us more than enough for ourselves and plenty left over to share with Bea and can or freeze. We modified a section of Pete's garage workshop to house chickens with a little outside run for them and had eggs almost daily. Even in the country, a fresh egg and clucking chicken in your backyard is welcome.

A cat started hanging around and we would feed it scraps, and one day Alice cut a hole in the old garage door just big enough to allow him to squeeze in and sleep up on the workbench. I was happy to have a mouser where we kept the chicken's grain.

Bea would stop in for dinner often and stay to play cards or watch television. We were volunteering at the local library where we'd help with fund raising and sorting donated books.

I had never been happier, never more contented, and never more in love. The journals sat in the drawer of my desk. I hadn't read or even thought about them for a while.

Yesterday, Alice and I worked out in the yard trying to get Pete's overgrown flower bed cleaned out. Pulling what we thought were weeds, and splitting clumps of perennials, mulching around them. The work was hard and dirty but satisfying, and when we stopped we could see the progress we had made and how good it looked. We took a break and sat on the front steps with a cup of tea to survey our progress when Michael's truck pulled into our driveway. I walked over to the cab as he rolled down the window and in a stern, angry tone said, "Listen, Sarah, you stay away from my property, my family and out of our lives. We know about you and what you're doing here with her. You're disgusting, both of you. You've broken Harry's heart and you have the gall to move in here and have her living with you. You're no different than your grandmother, you…"

I stood at the window with my mouth gaping, the experience eerily familiar, was it from the journal? We were both speechless for a second, but I recovered first. "I always knew that you didn't like us, but I never knew the extent of it." Without a pause I went on in a calm, but firm tone, "I will go about my business as always. Your family and property hold no interest for me. But I have a question for you, would you marry your cousin? Well I wouldn't, and no matter how much you may dislike me, we're related." I paused here for a moment and put an emphasis on the next word, "Uncle." He started to speak, but I charged on ignoring him, "So go and see if you can erase ME and the rest of us from your family tree. And if you don't know what I'm talking about, ask Harry."

Now, Michael was sitting there opened mouthed. Hesitating for just a moment before replying in a low, menacing voice, "You don't know what you're talking about. You'd better not start spreading ugly lies and rumors."

"You'd better learn your facts and leave us alone." I turned and walked back to the steps, and stood next to Alice, picked up my cup and sipped from it, watching him. He glared at us for a moment and then backed out of the driveway and slowly drove towards his house, head turning to look at us as long as he could.

"What was that about? It didn't look pleasant." Alice sipped her tea and watched Michael drive away.

The hand raising my tea cup to my mouth was shaking, my knees were feeling weak, and my heart was pounding. I'm not used to confrontations like that. I usually avoid unpleasantness, but this was to me, unavoidable. I sipped on my tea and went over the exchange in my mind, reviewing it as I spoke.

"He told us to stay away from his property and family, and that I broke Harry's heart. Can you believe it? So, I told him we weren't interested in his property or his family, and more or less said that that I would not marry my cousin. And that he was my uncle."

"Holy Cows, you said that?" Alice sat there with her cup midway to her mouth looking shocked. "Here, sit down, you look shook"

"Is that all he said?" Alice was trying to understand it as much as I was. "I know there are people in town who don't seem to like me, or don't like who they think I am. But no one is that outspoken, they just avoid me, which is fine with me. But this is like an attack, how ugly."

"Yeah, that was about it, but this could be trouble, you know Bea doesn't know about Doris and Pete and William. If she hears about it from Michael or he starts talking around… well it wouldn't be fair to her to hear it that way. I was never going to tell her, but now, I think I'll have to."

That evening I decided to finish the journals, in case there was anything more I had to know before I approached Bea with her history. I wondered if she had an inkling. If she had a clue that Doris was her mother, or that Michael was her half brother?

Chapter 51 – Rebecca

June, 1966

What an odd coincidence, as I was going through some old pictures and Doris's letters, I found my old diary, hidden in her drawer. Doris, my love, is gone. I cannot write this without emotion, the tears stream from my eyes and are staining the pages. Sometimes I have moments of peace, when I can look back and think that I could want nothing more, but the empty space next to me in the bed is so dreadful. A pang as sharp as a knife strikes me when at night I reach out and don't find her. The emptiness brings me to the sudden realization that she's not there and not coming back.

I was so selfish. I wanted her all for myself. But when I went off with Peter those times, I know I hurt her. I could only think of myself, I still regret that. I still think of the little things that I could have been more thoughtful of. But Doris was always forgiving of me always ready to let things go. She was the better of us. But I shouldn't punish myself. She always said that I was too hard on myself.

So now I've found my diary, how many years since those days at the mill. Could I ever have guessed during that tormented time that Doris and I would be living together and having a fine family? For indeed we do, we have a daughter and granddaughter, both beautiful and smart and caring. For that I am most fortunate. Doris and William had a fine son, but the daughter is ours, Doris', Peter's and mine. I was to be her mother, but I wasn't able to bear a healthy child, so Doris did, and because Peter and I were married she let me raise her as though she were mine. I raised her daughter. That was the kind of person Doris was, she accepted it, she suggested it, she knew that the only way we could be together in this little town was to seem like every other little family, a mother and father and maybe an aunt or cousin living in with them and their kids. And now Bea comes to see me with her daughter Sarah and I have to kiss them and be the mother and grandmother that they expect and know, all the while knowing that although I am their family, Doris is their blood.

When I look at Sarah I am fascinated to see her eyes, her hair, her expressions, they are so much like Doris's. She must think me a goofy old lady who just stares at her. She looks more like Doris than Bea does. She is almost the spitting image of Doris. Why Bea hasn't noticed or Sarah herself, I don't know. There are pictures of Doris and me and Peter around the house, but they don't seem to have made the connection, which I do every time I see them. It almost takes my breath away when Sarah runs up the front steps and pops in the door and yells, "Hey, Gram?" I am so thrilled to see them, for although they are not my dearest Doris, they are a part of her. I see glimpses of her in them, like catching her reflection in a wispily veiled mirror. I found this picture of Doris. We had it taken after the kids were born and she was feeling somewhat despondent. For some reason we got an offer for a photograph and we decided to have her picture with the kids and with her by herself. I just found it and she is so beautiful and I can see how very much Sarah resembles her. Of course the photographer pressed us to buy more photos, but we just took this one for a small fee.

This is all fresh and tender because they just left after a visit. I fixed them tea and had some cake, we all ate and laughed and talked until they had to leave and I am alone and lonely again. How empty it seems after they leave. After a week of eating my meals alone and knitting and reading the paper and puttering in the garden and going for a walk, I get a few hours of joy which I know will always end with an empty house. I selfishly wish that I had gone before Doris. I miss her so. Next month is my birthday. Bea and Sarah are going to take me out to dinner. If I have the energy, I'm going to get a new dress to go out with them. Bea's picking me up to go shopping tomorrow. Some things to look forward to.

Chapter 52 – Sarah

I decided to have Bea over to the house to tell her. Alice wanted to know if I thought she should be there or if she should go out for a while. It was such a sensitive subject. I didn't know if Bea would be more comfortable with just me or if Alice, who sometimes had a different and more insightful outlook than I, would help to give us perspective. We decided that Alice would go out to the store for a while when I started to talk to Bea, then return.

I called Bea and asked her over on Friday evening, telling her we were going to have a little dinner.

Friday came. We had a nice roasted chicken with small potatoes, beets and green beans, all vegetables from our garden. When I broke out the second bottle of wine, Alice left for the market to pick up a few essentials she said, against the protest of Bea who wanted to sit and gab with both of us for a while.

After Alice left, I brought in the diaries and pulled out the picture of Doris that had been folded into the last entry of Rebecca's diary.

"Nice picture, isn't it?" I handed it over to Bea who took it and glanced at it quickly.

"Yeah, when did you have your hair styled like that, I don't remember it?"

"Look again." I said with a leading tone. She stared at it, pushing her glasses up her nose, giving it more scrutiny. Then she looked at me and back at the picture. "Do you know who it is?"

"This isn't you, is it? It's Doris, isn't it? Goodness, the likeness is remarkable." She squinted down at the picture.

"Why do you think so? Why do I look so much like Doris and so little like Rebecca?"

"What do you mean?" Bea's voice cracked with a tense tone. She took another sip of sherry.

"Think about it, Mom, why do I look more like Doris than Rebecca? Why do I almost look like Doris's twin?"

"What are you saying; that DORIS is your grandmother? That's ridiculous." Bea's tone was shakily defiant.

"Not just my grandmother, but your mother." She stared at the picture, tipping her head to one side.

"My mother?" Bea drew the words out, squinting again at the picture, trying to pull the idea into a reality that she could embrace. Finally she replied, "My mother. Are you sure? This isn't a hoax?"

"The diaries tell it all. It's complicated, but the short version is that Rebecca and Pete married, but when she couldn't have children, Doris offered to. Since Pete and Rebecca were married it would have seemed improper for Doris to have the children – they pretty much kept her pregnancy a secret until the baby was born and then they told everyone the baby, you, were Rebecca's. Doris played the aunt."

"You know Doris was like my mother, they both were. But Doris would be more soothing when I was hurt or in trouble. I would go to her. Sometimes, if I did something that made Rebecca mad, I'd run to Doris and she'd tell me how they both loved me and to try not to make my mother mad. That's what she'd say – try not to make your mother mad – and she'd give me a big hug."

"Were there things that looking back now might have been clues?"

"I just don't know why I didn't see it before? Doris was the warmth in the house. They all were good parents, but Becky had a temper sometimes, and Pete was often busy with something else, either in the garden or visiting William, or puttering on something. But Doris, she was the rock, the always loving and steady rock." Bea paused to look at the picture again and sip the sherry that I'd served us. "So, when were you going to tell me?"

"Actually, I wasn't sure if I should tell you, if it was needed or if it would unnecessarily turn your world upside down. And remember when I first started reading the diaries you didn't want to know what was in them? Well I thought you meant it."

"So? Why are you telling me now?"

"Michael stopped by to harass us – telling us to stay away from his family and I told him he was our family. That's another part of the family story – Doris also gave birth to Michael by William."

"Come on," Bea said, emphasizing both words, sounding flabbergasted, as one would be hearing this story for the first time.

"Well, Doris's diary has it all. Do you think you want to read it now?"

"It sounds like a melodrama."

"Yeah, it probably does, but it's our melodrama."

Bea picked up the photo and stared intensely at it, then in a low voice addressed it, "Why didn't you tell me?" I watched her puzzle over it, brow furrowed, slightly shaking her head. Telling her was the right thing to do. I knew that as time went by, the answers would reveal themselves to her, that everyday would likely bring another revelation, more insight.

Just then the back door opened and in came Alice holding up another bottle of sherry. "Hi, do you need a little more of that sherry or are you ready for coffee?" She cheerfully put the bag down on the counter, looking from one of our faces to the other, trying to read what the climate was. The door closed as another person came in behind Alice, a smoky voice said, "Beatrice?" And a head peered around from Alice's shoulder.

Bea, really looked shook now and in an unsteady voice said, "Who's that? Cheryl? What's going on, are you girls trying to make me crazy?"

Cheryl stepped around from behind Alice and pulled Bea up and hugged her. Not letting go until Bea said, "Dammit, get me a tissue." Cheryl held her out at arm's length and said, "Geeze, you look great! I missed you so much."

Bea looked at her, wiping her eyes and then at me, "This is your doing, I'm sure." Then she looked to Alice and back to me, snorted and with a slightly angry tone said, "You've known all along too, huh? Well I'm glad we're all in these muddy waters together. What are you waiting for, get a couple more glasses and join the lunacy." But she said it with a smile.

Afterward

The era of the Mill Girls or Factory Girls in New England peaked between 1830 and 1870.

Much of the mill story in this novel is centered at the Willimantic Mills, which, unlike the story, did not run looms, but primarily handled cotton thread. Thread from the Willimantic Mills started with bales of cotton batting, to carding, to spinning, dyeing and finally it was wound onto bobbins. Because of their lower wages, women were a desirable source of labor for mills.

The older fictional memoirs in this novel were intended to take place during an era when some mill towns still had boarding houses for women. The Elms boarding house in Willimantic was build around 1865 and originally boarded women on the second floor and men on the third. As of this writing, the structure still exists although one story was removed when it was renovated to become an apartment house.

The Library from the older storyline still exists on the third floor of the Willimantic Textile Mill and History Museum. This had housed offices, a company store, and the library on the third floor.

Most of the information that the novel portrays about mill girls and boarding houses for women is based on information collected from various resources, some listed below.

Single women working at the mills during this era were required to stay at subsidized boarding houses. Most often these houses had bedrooms that had 2 to 4 double beds, which were shared by the girls. Girls often shared beds with sisters, cousins or friends, but were sometimes required to bunk with strangers. A few boarding houses had rooms with 2 single beds or one or two double beds. Most of them did not have much additional furniture as they were cramped and the women were required to keep their clothing and personal items under their beds in their band boxes, or in a dresser, if available.

Their days were long, often 12 hours or more. The references of bells calling them to work or to their meals and the requirements to be on time or get locked out, are factual. The requirement to go to church regularly is also factual, but not all companies required them to go to a proscribed church. They attended one of the many religious groups that flourished during this time, including the Unitarians, Quakers and other, more fringe religious sects.

The mill girls earned many times more than any other women workers of the time. Many women of that time found employment as teachers, seamstresses, domestics, laundry women or inn and boarding house keepers.Mill work gave women an independence they had not previously had, and allowed them a way to save and have extra cash to spend. Many towns grew rapidly around these mills. Stores and services were alluring to people with expendable income. Even though the mill girls made $2 to $6 per week (a grand sum during this time) they were still earning roughly half of what the male workers were earning. Many of these girls sent good portions of their salaries back home to help with a brother's education or family finances, while some saved for their own dowries. Imagine what independence this gave to women who were previously dependent upon men for everything.

Later, during the post-bellum era, when textiles mills were going through more difficult economic times, the mills lowered the pay and sped up the machinery. Groups of women sometimes went out on strike (or "turned out"), but usually the strikes did not succeed. To fight back, the mills stopped production in some sections or "scabs" were brought in, often under police protection, hired by the companies to break the strike. So workers either went back to work or lost their jobs.

To learn more about mill girls, check the resources below.

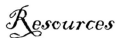

Resources

FARM TO FACTORY Women's Letters, 1830-1860 – Edited by Thomas Dublin – Columbia University Press, 1981

LIFE IN A NEW ENGLAND MILLTOWN – Sally Senzell Isaccs – Heinemann Library, Chicago, Illinois, 2003

WILLIMANTIC WOMEN: Their Lives and Labors – Tom Beardsley – Windham Testie and History Museum, 1990

LOOM & SPINDLE or Life Among the Early Mill Girls – Harriet H. Robinson – Press Pacifica, 1976

Elms Boarding House:

http://www.millmuseum.org/Mill_Museum/Elm.html

Company Store and Library:

http://www.millmuseum.org/Mill_Museum/Captains_of_Ind.html